The BONE SPARROW

'A contender for the children's book of the year ... a heartrending tale about how our stories make us, and also an angry polemic, vividly convincing in its detailed description of what it means for your home to be a tent in the dust behind a guarded fence' – *THE SUNDAY TIMES*

'Outstanding . . . This is an important, heartbreaking book with frequent, unexpected humour, that everyone, whether teenager or adult, should read' – *GUARDIAN*

'*The Bone Sparrow* is one of those rare, special books that will break your heart with its honesty and beauty, but is ultimately hopeful and uplifting' – *BOOK TRUST*

'The story of Subhi, sensitively told and immensely moving, gives us a glimpse of what a homeless, imprisoned existence life feels like . . . and how the hope invested in a vision of a better future can end up being the difference between making it out, and surrendering to despair' – *BIG ISSUE*

'This is a tragic, beautifully crafted and wonderful book whose chirpy, stoic hero shames us all. I urge you to read it' *INDEPENDENT*

'A special book' – *MORRIS GLEITZMAN, author of the acclaimed* Once *series*

'A profoundly poignant novel about what it means to live as a refugee' – *METRO*

'Zana Fraillon's powerful and poetic tale of friendship in the face of injustice will fly away with your heart' KATHARINE MARSH, Edgar Award-Winning *author of* The Night Tourist

'Moving and memorable, *The Bone Sparrow* deserves to be read by all who care about our common humanity' *SF SAID, judge of the Guardian Children's Fiction Prize, 2016*

'The writing is beautiful and the message of survival and bravery a universal one' – *THE BOOKSELLER*

'What a powerful story. Detention camps are no place for children. No place for humans' – *CLARE HALL-CRAGGS, BOOK TRUST*

'Think of it as a powerful polemic, yes, but also think of it as a story of the redeeming power of friendship and the vital nature of storytelling' – *BOOKBAG BLOG*

'This book made me cry in Temple Gardens at page 21. Loving it' – *GRASS FOR DINNER BLOG*

'So beautiful. And so important . . . encourages empathy. For kids and adults alike!' – *BOOK ADDICT BLOG*

ORION CHILDREN'S BOOKS

First published in Great Britain in 2017 by
Hodder and Stoughton

1 3 5 7 9 10 8 6 4 2

Text © Zana Fraillon, 2017

A CIP catalogue record for this book
is available from the British Library.

ISBN 978 1 5101 0158 6

Typeset by Input Data Services Ltd, Somerset

Printed and bound in Great Britain by CPI Group (UK) Ltd,
Croydon, CR0 4YY

The paper and board used in this book are from well-managed forests
and other responsible sources.

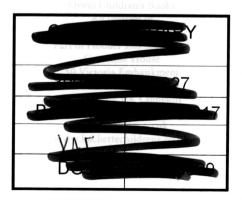

To all the silenced voices

There was a stirring in the mud. A soft rumble from deep in the riverbank that sent the fish swirling and stopped frogs mid hop. It was just a hint, a whisper, that something was coming. Something was about to begin.

Esra

My name is Esra Merkes. I am eleven years old. The tattoo on my arm says I belong to Him, Orlando Perel. It says the Snakeskins are my family for life. It says I am kept. It says I am owned. They think just because I close my eyes and shut my ears and follow their words, that I have forgotten who I am. They think I am theirs to make.

But that is not *my* truth.

No ink scratched in my skin can tell me who I am. No roughed hands and twisted faces can turn me soft. My truth is stronger than a thousand hands, and fiercer than a million twisted mouths.

I am Esra Merkes. They do not know me. They do not know I can wait. They do not know, one day, I will be free.

Curled on the floor, the stink of blood and sweat crawling up my nose, I tell my truth over and over, letting those words keep me whole. I tell my truth until the beating stops and the footsteps have gone back up the stairs, and the door has locked us in again and the pain has cooled off and the only sound left is Miran breathing *Sorry* over and over again in my ear.

'Suck it up, princess, I'm not dead yet,' I tell him, and wipe the blood from my mouth, and he smiles and wipes the wet from his eyes. I know he didn't mean to be late. 'Anyway, what doesn't kill me only makes me stronger, neh?'

Miran smiles and says, 'Or at least a little crazier.' Then he pulls me to a sit and we lean into each other, our shoulders warming at the touch of skin, the wet of the wall against our backs.

Miran reaches into his pocket and pulls out an orange. A real orange. It hurts my mouth to smile and it'll hurt more when that juice stings the cracks in my lips, but that orange is worth it. Miran takes some peel and puts it in my mouth. I let it sit on my tongue and suck at the flavour. The bitter bites right through the taste of blood and dirt, and for just a moment, I'm back home, sitting in the shade dipping orange peel into melted chocolate, my brother pulling faces at the taste. But it's only a flash of a memory. A shadow I can't catch.

'I don't think that's true anyway,' Miran says. 'There's lots of stuff that might not kill you, but definitely wouldn't make you stronger. Like a bear. Or a crocodile. Or a really angry duck.'

'A duck?'

Miran nods, not smiling even a bit. 'Ducks can be vicious. Have you seen those beaks? And their slappy feet? They pretend to be nice and cute, but you look in a duck's eyes, and all you will see is hate.'

I shake my head. 'Well, maybe not a duck then. Come on, tell me what it was like out there.'

'It was sunny,' Miran says, his eyes soft with remembering. 'Hot. I could smell the rain on the wind. I felt it on my face, those tiny drops. It didn't pour down though. I wish it had. My bones were aching for it, you know?'

I take another piece of peel and put it on my tongue. 'What else?'

Miran thinks. He's remembering being outside this room, outside this house, past the metal gates, out in the world, just for the day. I can see his face holding hard to keep each detail fresh. 'The people,' he says after a while. 'I forgot there were so many people. All those faces, Esra.'

I close my eyes, the skin pulling tight over the lumps growing fast on my face and tell myself to push through the hurt and listen. Miran is telling every little detail so I can imagine and fool my brain to believing I'm remembering too, as if I'd been out there, with him. That's the rule, whenever one of us is pulled to a job outside, we have to tell everything. They only ever pull one of us, leaving the other locked behind as guarantee. That way they know we won't try to run. We've seen what happens to the one locked behind if we do. We've seen what happens to the one locked behind if we don't do as we're told, or if we don't earn enough, or if we get picked up by police.

Or if we come back late . . . Miran looks at me. He's hurting worse than me, knowing my pain is on him.

'I'm sorry, Es,' Miran says again. 'I was thieving a wallet and my hand got caught in his pocket. He almost caught me. I had to run for ages to lose him, and—'

I put my hand on his knee. 'Forget it. It's nothing. You've always been rubbish at thieving wallets. You rush it too much.' I push him with my elbow. 'What else was there?'

He thinks a bit, his fingers pushing a piece of orange flesh, juiced and sweet onto my tongue. 'There was a fair. Full of clowns and rides and music and magicians, and I got to go on every ride three times and they fed me up on hot dogs and ice cream and—'

I push him with my elbow again. Now he's trying to fool his brain as well. 'For real, Miran. What else was there really?'

'There could have been a fair. Maybe there was and I just didn't see it.' He thinks a bit longer. 'I forgot how the light changes, you know? How it starts soft in the morning and gets hard and bright until its almost the end of day, and then the light turns to shadows and tricks your eyes into thinking you're seeing things. You can just about believe anything is possible in that light.'

The light never changes down here. In this room under the house, with its puddled floor and too bright lights, time doesn't even exist. There are no days or nights or hours down here, just an endless now.

The lights are kept on all day and all night for the plants. Burning hot lights that hang from chains from the ceiling and shine brighter than the sun. There are so many plants down here we call it The Jungle. More plants than we can count, hundreds of them, growing in rows in their pots all the way from one wall to the next, some just starting up from the dirt, others so big we can't see over all those leaves.

This room has been our world for eighty-four days now, Miran and me. Little Isa too, except he arrived on day 9, all wrapped up in that too big jumper of his that he won't take off no matter how hot. He spent most of the first week rocking himself in a corner, whimpering and shaking. 'He's aching,' Miran had said.

'He needs to grow up,' I told him. 'Orlando has no use for babies.' But we left Isa alone. He's not even seven years old, and too small to work much anyway. Orlando doesn't need to know Isa's not working yet.

Miran keeps track of the days by the sprinklers. They come on once in the morning and once at night to feed the plants and so we can fill our water bottles. Miran marks up a brick in the wall each time they start, smiling every time. He said when we get to one hundred days we should have a party. We laughed so hard, Isa thought something was wrong with us. He didn't get why it was so funny. He hasn't been around long enough I guess.

When they locked the door that first night, Miran

looked at the plants growing up around us, and he turned to me and said, 'What kind of tree can you carry in your hand?' I told him to shut up. Miran and his stupid riddles. Even still it took me all night to get it. 'A palm tree.' I woke him up to tell him.

Our job in The Jungle is to grow the plants up, to water them just right and move the fans around the room so each plant gets enough air blowing all over it. To wet the plants with a spray that stings our eyes, shakes our legs, catches in our throats, sends an angry rash up our arms, and puts the taste of metal in our mouths. To make sure this room stays just hot enough and just wet enough for the plants to grow strong, and to scrub any dot of mould from the walls so it doesn't get to a plant and make it sick. These plants we grow are worth a lot of money to Orlando. He trusts us to do it right. There are worse jobs than this.

Isa says these plants are for making medicine to stop people dying. Miran must have told him that lie, but it makes him happy, and he sings to every one of those plants and talks to them like they understand. He even has names for some of them. *'Hello Niri, so good to see you today. Are you feeling well?'* I don't tell him he's wrong, that these plants are turned to drugs which people buy so they can go crazy for a time. I don't tell him these plants are what feed the street rats and turn them to zombies. I don't tell him only because I like the sound of his singing.

When a plant is ready and the flowers change to just the right colour, we harvest it, and hang it in paper bags in the drying cupboard. That cupboard is the only space in here that isn't too hot. It's big and dry and cool with a breeze pushing through a tiny window from the outside. We aren't meant to spend long in the cupboard, but sometimes I sit in there, looking up at the window and letting the outside wind blow over me, and I close my eyes and imagine.

Unless we're pulled for a job, the only other time we leave this room is to load up one of the trucks with the bags of dried plants. That happened on days 11, 23, 41, 58, and day 67. Isa scratched at the brick to put a circle around those days like a sun.

The last time we loaded the truck, the boss said we had done good. He was old and greyed and had more tattoos covering over him then anyone I'd seen. He said he would tell Orlando that we were working hard. He gave us all a chocolate bar for free and let us sit outside in the front garden to eat. My eyes stung after being inside so long, but it was a good sting, and we smiled and felt the wind on our faces and the grass at our feet and the sun warming our heads.

Just down the street, a bus full of kids drove in to the school. I could hear them singing through the open windows. '*A duck walked up to a lemonade stand, and it said to the man, running the stand, hey, ba ba ba, got any grapes?*' They didn't look at us though. Just drove

7

past and into the school like we weren't even there. Like we were invisible.

No one here sees us for real. They just see the house looking like any other house in the street, with its brown bricks and blue curtains and wooden door with a Neighbourhood Watch sign stuck to the window. They just see three kids eating chocolate bars and don't think to even wonder. It's like Orlando says. Here, in this country, we don't exist.

That old, tattooed Snakeskin watched the bus, then he brought out cans of drink that dribbled down our faces and turned our hands sticky. 'No charge,' he told us. 'This is your reward for doing good.' He took a football from his truck and he kicked it to Isa, back and forth, his smile big enough to show his browned teeth clamped hard on his cigarette. But he kept looking at Isa. I've seen people look like that before, looking, like he had ideas to move Isa to a different kind of job.

Miran saw too. He squeezed my shoulder and closed his eyes. He tipped his head back and when the sun hit his face it turned it white and flat and empty like stone. I watched that man put his hand on Isa's head and rub at his hair. I watched him reach in his pocket for another chocolate bar and whisper in Isa's ear so Isa smiled up at him, believing.

Miran's eyes were still closed when I stood up. He didn't see me kick that ball on to the road and kick the side of the man's truck so it left a dent the size of my heel in the door. He didn't see me grab Isa by his jumper. He heard me though, telling that man to jam his chocolate bar. He saw me spit at his feet and he followed when I pulled Isa back inside the front door, all the way along the hallway with its flowered carpet and back down the stone steps into The Jungle, Isa not saying a word the whole time, but tears tracking dirt down his face.

And when the man followed us into The Jungle, his keys jangling and smiling through the smoke of his cigarette, Miran couldn't do a thing but put his arms around Isa and turn him away.

The man walked down the steps, slow and sure, all the way through the plants to where I stood at the back wall. He grabbed my cheeks in his hand, the keys pushing into my skin and he squeezed hard, his face up close to mine and his breath, all sour and smoked, pushed inside my nose and mouth and all the way into my chest.

'Be careful, girl,' he said, his voice growling like Orlando's dogs. 'Most people won't tolerate a mouth like that. Better hope I don't tell Orlando he needs to shape you up. Better hope I don't tell Orlando he should sell you on. I know people who would pay a good price for a girl like you.' Then he jammed my face into the bricks and held it there, watching. He took the cigarette from his mouth and moved it right up close to my face. I could feel the heat of it, the choke of the smoke. But I didn't move, didn't call out. I wouldn't let him win, no matter what he did. *They do not know I can wait.* After a time he let go and left, slamming the metal door to the The Jungle and locking it up tight. We heard him laughing as he walked down the hall.

But I won. Because he didn't come back for Isa. He didn't say a word to Orlando either because next time Orlando came to check on the plants and bring us our food He didn't say a word against me. Instead He told us we'd done good. He said if we keep doing good he'll give us a raise and we'll have paid back our debt before we know it. And we smiled, standing tall and proud that He'd noticed.

Orlando, He soft holds with the same hand that slaps us down hard. That same mouth that spits His anger like fire, can smile and kiss the tops of our heads so gentle we turn weak as babies, and all that fear we've got waves over us, and we feel our fingers hold hard to His shirt and feel our faces pressed against His chest, listening to His heart beating strong over us and breathing in His smell of sweat and smoke and petrol, and feeling sure and safe because He's looking out for us. Because we're Snakeskins. We're His, and He'll take care of us. And when His fingers trace over our tattoos, all we feel is proud.

After, we don't look each other in the eye for a long while, knowing how easy we were played.

On those days, I don't whisper my truth at all.

*

10

'One night,' Miran tells us, 'we will stand in the wild, and the river will lead us home. We will be free and happy, and that is when our living will begin.' This is how his stories start, every time. His Tomorrow Stories, he calls them. 'Might be tomorrow, might be the next tomorrow, might be a tomorrow far from now. But it will be a tomorrow, because it sure as hell isn't today.' And when he said it that first time, we laughed until tears ran down our faces.

Miran tells other stories too, old fairy stories like the ones his jidu told to him when he was little, but his Tomorrow Stories are the really good ones. Every time Miran tells a Tomorrow Story, he sits with his back straight, his fingers playing at the black string bracelet wrapped around his wrist, and he whispers us up a different tomorrow, each one blazing and bright and real enough that we can just about see our futures hanging in the air, waiting for us to catch up.

Back when Orlando first chose us, when it was us and a whole bunch of freshies scared and crying all night, Miran would shush away everyone's fear with his Tomorrow Stories. The Whisperer, we called him, and we believed his words, every single one. He's like that, Miran – he can make anyone believe anything just by saying it.

Miran has always been with me. Whispering me through every job, every boss, every beating. Right since that very first journey over in the truck, when were still fool enough to think we were finally going to a safe place after all the running, and hiding from the bombs and guns and soldiers and death. That must have been close to three years ago now.

We sat in that truck and talked on about the school we'd be going to, and how we'd come back smarter than anyone and richer than a thousand kings. We talked of the easy jobs we'd be working on weekends, and all the money we'd make to send back to our families. Of how each night our stomachs would ache with the fullness of food and how we'd forget that we'd ever known the bite of hunger or the scream of thirst. We talked of real beds and warm blankets, of hot drinks and a city full of books and wonders, waiting for us to find.

But when the truck stopped, Orlando and his boss men were waiting for us, cigarettes smoking, bottles in hands, and eyes as hard as the rock sharp ground we were thrown on. Orlando stomped all over our talk with His silver tipped boots. He showed us how much we all owed, the thousands and thousands of dollars, more money than our families had ever known. We owed Him for every sip of water we'd taken, and every crumb we'd eaten on the way here. We owed for the cost of coming to this country, for the truck's petrol and the driver and the clothes and blankets given us, and the space on the floor we'd slept. He showed how we were to pay Him back every bit, by hard work and hard hours all day every day. He showed what happens when we don't work hard enough, or fast enough. He showed pictures of those who ran and were hunted back down. He showed pictures of their families.

Then He smiled His smile and He held the ones crying, and poured food in our hands and warm tea in our cups. 'Now stop crying,' Orlando told us. 'You all agreed to come. Did you think I would pay for all of that? Did you think all this was for free?' And Orlando and His bosses laughed at the craziness of our thinking.

We did not move. We did not speak. We had all of us been fooled. It was our doing that brought us here with money owing, and every one of us felt that shame and guilt falling heavy and hard.

Then they covered our heads with those moulded sacks and burnt those tattoos in black pain on our arms and when I cried out with the fear and hurt of it all, Miran's fingers found mine and squeezed tight, promising to do all of it together.

But Orlando looks after us. He stops the police from locking us in their jails, and the other gangs from beating on us. He feeds us and buys us clothes and stops us from turning into street rat kids and starving in the dark like a dog. No matter what job us kept kids do, nothing is as bad as being a street rat. No one looks out for them, and soon enough they end up dead and wasted and rotting in the gutter. I've seen it.

Orlando won't let that happen to us. He grows us up. Those other gangs don't look after their kept kids like Orlando looks after us. Those other gangs get rid of their kids as soon as they get too weak, or too mouthy, or too old, and then you never see those kids again. Sometimes they get sold on, or taken to the Organ Boys, but mostly they end up just the same as the street rats. Food for the gutter dogs and no one to care whether they're living or dead.

And Miran and me know how to work hard and smart and stay strong until the day we buy our way free. We've done the hard jobs already. All the restaurants and massage parlours and nail bars and berry farms. And the factories where we sewed those life vests that drowned people faster than if they weren't wearing anything at all. And the houses where they fed us on bread all blue with mould because they figured good food would spoil us and give us ideas. That was when Miran started with his riddles. *'What do poor people have, and rich people want, and if you eat it, you die?'* He didn't even wait for me to work it out. *'Nothing!'* he answered, and laughed until the footsteps came to warn us to keep quiet. It was a stupid riddle though. Rich people want stuff all the time.

But we're working our way up, just like Orlando promised we could. Here in The Jungle we have enough food, as long as we ration the boxes Orlando brings in every week without fail. Here there are no babies to look after or meals to cook or nails to paint or floors to scrub. Here there are no visitors. Here, we even have

14

time free to do whatever we choose.

At first, we just slept, like cats curled on our blankets on the floor. But there's a danger to sleeping too much. It makes you soft. It dulls you. Sometimes we play hide and seek in the plants, and once every ten sprinkler-starts, we hide pictures on the walls. Back home I had a book with pictures of a crab hidden on each page and I'd spend hours looking, trying to find that tiny little crab. My abbi bought the book for me one time when we were driving on holiday. There are no books in The Jungle, and no pencils either, so we scratch pictures into the bricks with rocks. We have to try and find each other's picture before the next ten sprinkler-starts, but it can take ages to find them hidden behind the plants. Isa is always asking for clues but that's cheating. I tell him to look harder.

Sometimes when he's searching, he finds my words instead. The words that prick at my head and itch at my fingers and don't let up until I scratch them out and set them loose. I must've left a whole trail of words behind me, scratched on the walls of The Jungle and the houses before that and on the signs in the street and the bark of trees. Scratched out on anything just to free them from my skin and let me know I still exist.

Once, on day 54, Isa found a different picture in the bricks. One we hadn't drawn. This was a picture left behind. It's a good picture too. Of an octopus, with squiggly legs and big eyes, and floating above the octopus on curly waves is a boat and there are two people in the boat, one big and one small and they are looking down at the octopus and smiling.

'*What has seas but no water, forests but no trees, cities but no buildings, and can lead you free?*' Miran said when Isa showed us the picture. Isa and I didn't bother thinking up an answer. Instead we searched all over, looking for any more pictures left from those kids. If there are any more, we haven't found them yet. Maybe the kids got moved on before they could draw any more. Or maybe this picture is like my words and not a game at all.

Sometimes, when the others are asleep, I sit in front of the picture and try to imagine that I drew it. I try to imagine that it's my memory there on the bricks and not someone else's. I wonder where that kid is now. I wonder if he still remembers, or if he stopped drawing and lost his way. Memories are like that, once you forget, you can't ever find your way back. Thinking of that was when I worked out Miran's riddle. 'It's a map isn't it?' I told him, but he pretended that it had taken me so long to figure out that he'd forgotten what the riddle was in the first place.

The best part of working The Jungle is that our nights are free. No one bothers us here at night, and we can sleep without worrying about being woken for a single thing. We lie on our blankets and look up at the leaves and we talk of home. But we only talk about before the war. Of the days when we were little and nothing was wrong. Isa doesn't talk of home much. The home Isa remembers is the broken shell. The greyed, cracked city, her skin already torn from her bones.

He doesn't remember the coloured tiles in the city squares, or the green of trees against the blue sky. He doesn't remember the smell of the markets with the spices all piled up high, and the soft fabrics with stories woven into them. He doesn't remember the ringing of bikes and the warm hot of bread taken straight from the oven. He doesn't remember the fountains we dipped our feet in on hot days and the beaches where we'd go in summer. Isa never knew the real country. But he listens to us talk, and I tell him to close his eyes and remember, and he nods and says, 'I remember. I do.'

But then, every god damn night, Isa tells us over again what his abbi told him. *'Tears of a bull will set you free.'* Those words were the last his abbi ever spoke, right before he went and bit his own tongue off. His abbi must've been crazy, but little Isa has held tight to those words ever since he got here. 'I didn't even need setting free, back then,' Isa says, like that makes a difference.

Every night Isa tells the same damn story, and every night Miran smiles at him and says how wonderful, and that Isa's abbi must have been some kind of magic man to see into the future like that. Every night I roll my eyes and shake my head at the foolishness of it. And then, every night, Miran talks of his family.

I don't. Not ever. My family are all dead and gone, and no amount of talking will change that. But Miran's aren't. Maybe that's why Miran smiles when he marks up the bricks after each sprinkler. Maybe he's already thinking of his family.

It was games, stories, and whispers of home that used up the hours between working. But then, when Orlando came to check on us last week, when He said how good we'd done, He gave us a pack of cards. He said it was a reward for looking after the plants so well. He held it out to us in his hand, and when Isa reached for it I had to grab his arm to stop him taking it. Isa doesn't know that rewards can cost money. That just by taking it, our debt can get higher, so that all our work down here turns to nothing. He doesn't know how to work hard and smart so he can pay off his debt and buy his way free. If we don't teach him, he'll be owned forever.

Orlando bent down when I grabbed Isa's arm, His face close to mine. My eyes fell to the floor. He took my chin in His hand and raised my head until I was looking right at Him. 'Don't you trust me, girl?' He asked, and the softness of His voice sent iced shivers up my neck and shook at my knees. I didn't move. Didn't answer. He let go of my chin then and messed my hair and laughed.

'Good girl,' He said to me. 'Nothing is ever for free. You'll make a good boss one day, don't forget that,' and I felt my chest swell with pride and a powerful strong, before I remembered that I don't want to be a boss, that

I won't ever be a boss, that one night, we will stand in the wild, and we will follow the river home, and I'll get far away from Orlando and His Snakeskins before He fools me into becoming something I'm not. We won't be able to wait for Isa. He'll take too long to pay out his debt. We haven't told him yet.

Orlando ran His fingers, slow and gentle, along my tattoo then, and I closed my eyes. 'You, my girl, are just like me,' He whispered, so those words hissed hot in my ear. Then Orlando gave the cards to Isa and went to check the drying cupboard. I stood there with my legs shaking until Miran came and squeezed my fingers, and whispered 'One night . . .' and I remembered again who I am.

We don't know how much those cards cost us. Maybe they really are a gift, a reward for doing well. Maybe it's to show we really are moving up.

When Orlando left, we waited and listened. We waited until His footsteps thumped their way into the kitchen and out the back door. We listened to Him throwing food for the dogs and heard the sound of the back gate closing. And when the roar from His motorbike had gone, we smiled.

We took turns holding the cards and breathing in their smell, fresh from the box. We played all the games we could remember and made up fresh new ones and I magicked Miran's card to disappear and fly under a plant all the way on the other side of The Jungle, and I showed Isa how to build up towers of cards. I used to be great at building card towers. My brother and I would sit on the rug at our teta's and build card towers, higher and higher while our ummi and teta would talk and drink tea.

I didn't even care when Miran hassled us with another of his stupid riddles. '*I am always there, but no one can see me. I can be held onto, but never touched. If you lose me, nothing will matter. What am I?*'

I couldn't think of the answer. I didn't care much either because I had just built my card tower four stories high.

'I give up. What is it?' Isa asked, but Miran wouldn't tell.

'There's no giving up,' he said instead.

'Here, I've got one, Isa,' I told him. 'What is annoying, can't thieve wallets or build card towers, and comes up with stupid riddles?' And when Isa's laugh knocked down my tower, Miran smiled at me and it didn't matter at all any more how much those cards cost us. Right then, they were worth every cent.

It was because of the cards that we didn't notice.

Miran had remembered a new game called Pig. We were playing and Miran was laughing because no matter how hard I tried I always ended up the pig. But our job is not to play. Our job is not to laugh. Our job is to look after the plants.

Sometimes, something goes wrong with one of the wires from the lights and a fire can start. When we got moved to The Jungle, we were told this had happened before.

'A waste,' the boss had said. 'They were real nice those last kids.'

We were told to watch the wires and to check them. We were told how to put the fires out with the fire blankets and were shown how to fix wires that had burnt through by cutting them fresh and twisting them together again. We had to show we knew how to do it, and the boss showing us nodded and smiled and gave us his leftover fish and chips. He said it was leftover, but there were two whole bits of fish wrapped in foil and a whole parcel of chips. 'I guess I wasn't hungry,' he said when he saw me looking. But his eyes were nice. 'No charge,' he said. 'They're only leftovers, kid.'

So we did as he said. We watched the wires. We checked them, and there was no fire, not in the whole ninety-two days we'd been here. But I guess we didn't watch hard enough or check properly, and because we were playing Pig we didn't see the fire when it started.

Isa noticed first, screaming and pointing at the flames. They were already grown up taller than he was, licking and spitting at the cupboard with its dried up plants in paper bags. Then the whole thing went up, just like the bonfires back home when we would jump the coals and make a wish.

I saw the fire and knew then that we would die. We'd be turned to nothing but ash like those other kids. We would have been too, except right at that very moment, the sprinklers came on, like they'd been watching the whole time and were coming on just to save us. I pulled the hoses from the sprinklers and fired at the flames and Miran beat them down with the fire blanket and somehow we did it. And we were so glad, so happy we had put out the fire with nothing more than a few burns on our hands and feet to show for it, that we didn't even think to be checking and pulling the wires from the water all in puddles on the floor. We didn't think to be filling our water bottles in case.

We just smiled at each other, and when the water sparked at the wiring and the fans stopped turning and the sprinklers stopped sprinkling I felt that panic start in my stomach and pull at my chest. I guess those sprinklers weren't saving us after all.

We tried to fix it. We tried to fit the hoses back to the sprinklers and to cut the wires and twist them back clean. But those sprinklers and those fans stayed off, and there wasn't a thing to do but sit and wait.

Miran kept walking to the bricks and touching at the marks he made each day on the wall. But without those sprinklers, there's no knowing time. There's just the plants curling over, their leaves dropping, and our own mouths getting thicker and harder with thirst. With no sprinklers, there's no water for us either.

We drank the puddles from the floor and scooped what we could into the water bottles to ration. And when that ran dry, we sucked up water from the toilet. But the toilet must be connected to the sprinklers because it won't fill back up. It's almost empty, and now Miran and I won't drink at all. Just a sip when the thirst gets too bad. We save the water for Isa. He's too little to know thirst this bad. His body wouldn't know how to live.

'What about the plants?' Isa asked. 'They're too dry. They need something.'

I don't know whose idea it was, to spray the plants with the spray that kills the bugs, but to give them extra. I think it was mine. We figured that at least the plants could drink the spray. So we sprayed them all, kept spraying them, waiting for their leaves to pick up just a bit. We kept spraying even though it hung in the air and made our throats burn until we coughed and vomited and shook on the ground. But the spray just killed those plants faster than not having any water at all.

Our job is to make sure nothing goes wrong, to look after the plants. These plants we grow, they're worth a lot of money to Orlando.

We heard the truck arrive. Heard the footsteps in the hallway, the scratch of metal in the lock. And when that door opened at the top of the stairs, the boss turned his eyes along those rows and rows of curled, dead plants and the drying cupboard, burnt black and empty. He looked at us, his eyes turning hard and his hands shaking anger and fear at knowing what Orlando would do, and we saw our fate written there in his eyes.

This Snakeskin boss, he wasn't old like the other tattooed one. He didn't have nice eyes like the fish-and-chip boss. This one was just new at being a boss. Just grown enough to have paid out his debt and started earning for real. Too new to let us make a mistake.

His hand gripped tight to the bat he was holding. He reached for the chains. Walked down those stairs.

'There was a fire . . .' Miran said, his voice choking his throat.

'We didn't burn up and die. We put it out,' Isa said.

'It was an accident,' Miran whispered.

But we saw into his eyes and we saw how the boss had already turned more monster than man. He wasn't hearing a word, only the roaring in his own ears. I know because all I could hear was the roaring in my own ears. And Miran closed his eyes and turned his face empty as stone and didn't even call out with hurt when the bat broke him into the ground. And when that monster put down the bat and took out a knife, silver and shining from his pocket, Miran kept his eyes closed and I could see his lips moving, telling his own truth over and over to himself and silent as death.

But Isa, he screamed. He screamed and screamed and screamed and that monster turned to him, his chain raised high with an anger so fierce, and—

24

The roaring in my ears was so loud. So, so loud. Isa is too little to know pain that bad. His body wouldn't know how to live.

The roaring got louder.

So here we are now. Day 95. And over in the corner, there's the dark, wet-black and quiet. The air is thick and heavy, and Miran keeps shaking me, telling me we have to *get from here*, and pulling so hard at my arm that all the pain my brain forgot comes crushing back, and it's all I can do not to hit out at him and make him stop.

I need to move these plants. To pile them high in the corner so I don't have to see. They pull from the dirt, their leaves sticking to me like skin. I drop them in the corner, covering over that heavy black, burying it deep so I never have to think of it again. The silver knife twitches at me from the floor, the handle wet and slimed. I wipe it on my shirt and see my eyes shining back in the blade. I feel the sharp of it against my finger, the pull of my skin opening and the hot as a line of blood runs free. I fold the blade into the knife and put it in my pocket. It is mine now, this knife.

'Esra, please—' and now Miran's voice is a whisper and his eyes are aching all his pain and fear and want right at me. He holds my hand, squeezing my fingers, promising like always to do it together, and I turn my back on that corner and squeeze back.

Isa is under a table. He's rocking back and forth, sucking on his sleeve, and shaking so hard he looks near to breaking. 'Come on, Isa.' But Isa just pushes his eyes shut tight and wraps his arms around his ears.

'Tears of a bull . . .' he's saying, over and over. 'Tears of a bull will set me free.'

My eyes flick to the wall behind Isa, to my words scratched deep into the brick. *We are the ones that disappeared.* And my words shout at me to run. This is our Tomorrow, right now, and if we don't run now, we won't ever see that river. There is no safety in being a Snakeskin anymore. If Orlando finds us, we're dead. The only way out is to run as hard and fast as we can, from Orlando, from the other gangs, from the street rats, from the police. Run and never stop.

'So stay,' I tell Isa. 'Wait for your damn bull. But we're going.' I mean it too.

Miran unwraps Isa's arm and puts it over his own shoulder. 'I've told you that story, neh? The one about the bull who cried a whole river of tears?'

Isa stops rocking. He breathes deep and looks to Miran with those eyes full of hurt and hope all smashed in together. He shakes his head, and Miran stands him up, his voice calm in Isa's ear, blooming that story to get Isa out of here. I wrap my arm around Miran's waist, the three of us holding each other up.

My chest screams with every step I take and Miran's arm is dangling the way no arm should dangle, his leg dragging wet trails across the floor. We don't look in the corner. We don't look anywhere but through the metal door waiting at the top of the stairs, still open a scratch and the light whispering us from the other side. Miran keeps telling his story, Isa concentrating on each word, his eyes pinched closed like when he's trying to remember the home he never knew.

We start up the stairs, and I look back down at The Jungle. We never did make one hundred days.

We're almost at the top step when we hear it. The rumble outside. Getting closer, louder. It's Him. Orlando. His motorbike speeding to the back fence, that rumble turning to quiet in the lane. Miran stops and that fear runs wild across his face.

The lock turns in the back gate. The gate scrapes the ground and smashes at the fence. The dogs' chains bash, and they start up their crazy loud barks. Isa doesn't need a story to push him on now. We're up the stairs, through the metal door, into the hallway with its flowered carpet and black stains, and the dirt outside crunches under Orlando's black boots. Those heavy stomping soles and sharpened silver tips. A dog that didn't move quick enough yelps with His boot finding ribs. And those footsteps too strong to run from crunch closer.

We're running down the hall. Tripping, standing, falling, leaving a trail of handprints in black red blood on the white walls. Isa is moaning. I clamp my hand hard across his mouth, his eyes scatting.

Orlando's keys scratch at the lock in the back door and we hear the squeal of it swing open into the kitchen. Orlando is inside. We aren't going to make it. The keys smash down hard on the bench. We freeze. We hear the fridge open. We hear a bottle scrape the shelf and the lid twist off and roll along the floor where it's dropped. Orlando's fingers tap the bench. All He needs to do is open that kitchen door and turn into the hallway. All He needs to do is take three more steps and He'll see us. Standing here, stuck.

We're at the front door. Silent. Slow. Too slow. Too loud. Our fingers pulling at the locks, scrabbling at the wood, pulling at the handle. Silent. Slow. Too slow. Too loud.

Orlando's fingers stop tapping. The bottle slams hard on the bench.

There's quiet. He's listening. He's heard. The front door swings open in our hands, and we step through into the garden.

The dogs bark.

Miran pulls the door shut behind us, and the thud of it thumps fear through my gut. Those footsteps are coming fast and hard through the kitchen and down the hall, His eyes seeing that metal door hanging open, seeing The Jungle with all its dead plants, seeing into the corner, following our handprints to the door.

We didn't make it. We got so, so close. Thirty seconds sooner and we could have done it. We could have been

28

over the front gate and down the street. That's all we needed. Thirty more damn seconds. There are all those parked cars we could have hid behind, or the gardens we could have run into. We could have made it to the school on the other side of the road. Thirty more seconds and we could have got to the end of the street. We could have crossed that one big road, and then we would have been in the wild with all the trees and bushes and logs to hide us and keep us safe. *One night, we will stand in the wild, and—* Thirty seconds was all we needed.

Those heavy-strong and hard angry steps are all the way at the door now. The lock clicks. Miran and I grab the handle, but He's pulling and pulling and we're not strong enough. Never strong enough to fight Him.

Miran's eyes are crazed and his breathing is scatting in and out so fast and my head is shaking and someone is howling and screaming sorry to Orlando through the door, screaming that it was an accident and we'll pay and we're sorry, needing Orlando to say it's all OK, that we're forgiven, that we're His Snakeskins and He'll look after us and keep us safe, and needing more than anything for Him to pull us back inside and hold us tight, and I hear those howled words begging and pleading and I think, that voice howling, I think that's me.

A police car slow drives around the corner, its lights flashing, turning the white of the truck to red and blue and back again. That truck, still waiting at the gate with its doors hanging wide and no driver left to drive it.

'Tears of a bull . . .' Isa is rocking again, back and forth, his eyes pressed shut.

Orlando sees the police. Sees the lights flashing through the windows, sees the car through the eyehole in the door. He stops pulling at the handle. He won't be found here. Not with us. Not with The Jungle. Not with the dark in the corner. Orlando is too clever. He won't ever be found, and all of it, all of everything down there in The Jungle, will be on us.

These police will lock us up and leave us to rot, just like Orlando said they would. *People in this country don't want criminals like you running around. There's a war on crime, a war on you. The police want to lock you away so they can say they are doing their job,'* Orlando told us, and he gave us all a number to call if the cops ever picked us up. The number that brings us straight back to Him, with more owing from getting us out of those jails and disappearing us from the police and the judges all doing their jobs.

But that number's not for us now, and being in jail just means waiting for one of Orlando's men to find us. Orlando has men everywhere. Jail just means we've nowhere to run.

We hear Orlando breathe out thick and close, that growl from His throat that ices the blood in my veins. 'Please,' I say. There's nothing but quiet, then His fist thumps hard on the door, cracking the wood, and I feel my piss run hot down my leg. We aren't forgiven. That thump is His promise. He'll find us. Out here. In their jails. On their streets. Wherever we are, He'll find us. And when He does—

Orlando snaps the locks on the inside of the door. We hear His footsteps thump back down the hallway, away from the police, away from us. We hear the metal door to The Jungle slam close, those locks clicking. We hear the back door smash shut and the dogs still barking. The motorbike thunders its roar down the back lane, and He's gone, He's left us and I put my hand over Isa's mouth to stop his whimpering before I see it isn't Isa whimpering at all. It's me.

Our hands fall from the door, Miran's eyes wide and mouth sucking at the air.

I squeeze Miran's fingers. We're never walking through this door again. And for just a second, the whole world stops and waits, holding us there outside of that house, letting the cold from the wind slap the fear from our brains and the warm of the sun kiss away every tear still stubborn enough to wet our cheeks.

The smell from the fire hangs in the air still, sticky and sour, and I watch the curtain pull shut in the house across the road. I wonder if it was her that called the police. I wonder if it was because of the smell, that smoke telling everyone what's been growing down there under that house. Maybe it was the truck stopped on the path, no driver and waiting too long. Maybe it was the screams stealing through that opened metal door. Maybe it wasn't her at all.

'Hiya, kids.' The police smile as they pull from their car. We aren't fooled. There's two of them, radios buzzing and hands on belts, their sticks itching at their fingers.

'God damn police,' Miran says. I spit on the ground so the police know we've got them worked out, so they know we won't be tricked, and lean Miran and Isa backwards, away from the car and away from the men in their too clean uniforms, slow walking up to the gate, their eyes judging how much wild dog we have in us.

But Miran won't pull. His head shakes slow.

'Miran, come on. This is our Tomorrow, neh? They've nothing on us. They're just a couple of fat, soft uniforms.' We've outrun fitter police than these before. They still need to haul their too big arses over the locked up gate, and down the path with its grown over weeds and crooked up bricks waiting to catch at their boots. We can get up and over the side fence before they even get close. They don't have the speed we do.

But Miran won't move. He drops his arm from my shoulder and pushes me back. His eyes lock on mine, and his fingers tie a knot in his shirt. '*With our souls tied together, we won't ever be apart,*' he whispers.

Those words, they kept me going once when I was fresh off the truck and no more than a baby, Miran's voice playing in my head every time we were separated. We'd tie knots in our shirts, and whisper those words, and every time we'd make it back together just like those words promised. Like it was some kind of magic spell keeping us together and safe. But I was just a baby then. Too little to know better.

'Don't be stupid, man—'

'Get.' He says it soft, but that word falls rock hard. He looks at his broken up leg. The rotten fruit on the ground bleeds between his toes and turns his foot a purpley red and black as blood. He looks back at me, then with his good arm, picks up a branch fallen fresh from the tree, all thick and heavy in his hand.

Those police stop, and thumb open their belts, their sticks up and ready, their voices cooing out to 'Take it easy now kids, we just want to talk to you is all.' But Miran and me have been around too long. We've heard those coos and those words too many times before, we've seen the blank that covers their eyes and we sure as hell know how hard those sticks fly.

'Take Isa.' Miran's voice is strong and sure, his hand gripping hard at the branch. He's talking to me but his eyes are on the police trying to creep forward without us seeing.

'I'll find you, just like always, and then we'll follow the river and go home. But go now. Isa's too little . . .' He looks at me quick, his eyes fighting back all the fear and sad pushing at us both. 'Tie your knot Esra,' he says.

Stupid knot won't do a damn thing of good. Stupid knot means nothing. But still my fingers shake, gathering up the fabric and twisting it tied at my hip.

'Now get,' he sniffs, and before I can answer no, before I can tell him I won't, he turns to those police trying to open the gate, and before I can stop him, he's limping their way, swinging the branch and snarling, letting them see for real how much fierce is still in him.

I want to stop him. I want to wrap him round my shoulders and force him away. I want to walk next to him, branch in hand, wild dog ready. I want to face all of everything together, just like always.

But I don't. I take Isa, and we scat to the side fence, away from the police, away from Miran, pulling ourselves up the vine curled to the wood, the pain cutting at my chest and Isa's hand gripped tight to my shirt. I turn back once, right on top of the fence. Miran is setting everything ever in him loose. He's taking all that anger and fear and hurt, and is flying it free, keeping those police back behind the front gate. Those police are itching at hauling us back to answer. But Miran won't let them.

One of them pulls to a crouch on top of the gate, his stick raised high, ready to crack down hard. 'Miran!' My scream throws the birds from the trees and unsteadies the crouched up cop. His eyes leave Miran and find me instead, just for a second. But that police never reckoned on how fast Miran has learnt to be, even broken like he is. His branch hits, square on an arm, and I hear a crack and see the surprise in that police's eyes.

There won't be any stopping them now. Miran turns his back on them then, the branch loosed and dropped from his fingers. His eyes find mine, frozen on the fence, and they tell me to run.

I don't see them take Miran down. I hear them though. The grunts and the thuds. Seems there's wild dog in everyone.

We're over the fence, Miran's eyes pushing us faster, and then we're through another fence and cutting through a garden with a boy playing in his tree house, flying a flag in the wind. He waves at us and claps when we run past. Isa waves back. Then we're out on the road, racing between cars screaming all around us, and our bare feet scraping skin against the hot black. We're heading straight for the river and the wild to cover us up and hide us and keep us safe.

I reckon I can hear boot steps chasing us down, but my own breathing's heavy in my ears and the fear gets louder and louder, pumping through me. We keep on running, through the park and into the wild, going faster and faster over the rocks and sticks cutting up our feet and pulling at our legs, through the thorns grabbing at our shirts and tearing pain through our skin.

It's the fear that keeps us going, pounding along next

to the river, slipping in the mud, running until the sun is barely pushing through the trees.

I fall in the mud then, Isa pulled on top of me, his arms wrapping around my neck. I suck in as much of that river water as I can, drinking so fast I choke and heave it back up, then I just sit there, blank and empty. I don't even notice that I'm lying in my own vomit or that my shorts are cold with piss, or that the sting in my eyes is from blood dripping from my head. I don't even notice when Isa's closed his eyes, and we've been lying so long that the day's turned to night and I'm wet and cold with river water shaking right through me.

I look at Isa, dreaming of that crying eyed bull of his, no doubt. I want to wake him, to tell him that his abbi was wrong. That it wasn't a bull that set him free. It was Miran. Small and broken and too bone tired for this world. I want to tell him so he never forgets.

This isn't the way it's supposed to be. This isn't how free is supposed to feel. This is just the same as always, except now Miran isn't here to dream with. This isn't my truth, and if this is what I've been reaching for this whole time then I'm the fool. Because this free I've got right now, this feels a whole damn lot like fear.

It's the moon that wakes me. The light cutting through the black to pull my eyes wide. I haven't seen the moon for a long time. I forgot how big and bright it can get. When my brother and I were small, my teta used to point up to the night sky, and she'd sing out a song in that river water voice she had, '*Please let the moon that shines on me, shine on the ones I love.*' But I learnt a long time back, that moon doesn't listen to a word of song.

Isa's curled on top of me, awake and watching, and when he sees my eyes open he smiles at me through his sleeve, and leans his head back on my chest.

All around, there's that wild, deep black and towered tall, the dark of the night turning trees to beasts and rocks to waiting men, my ears twisting every rustle of bushes to Orlando and his bosses. And suddenly, I want to be back in The Jungle, back safe and looked after, with its walls keeping us from harm and Miran whispering me into Tomorrow.

The tattoo on my arm starts to burn, and I scratch at the black snake rising up along my wrist, its long body twisting around the letters *O P*. Orlando Perel. Orlando will have every boss crawling all over looking for us. Every Snakeskin will have our faces to look out for. We're the hunted now, just like in those photos He showed us.

I whisper my truth, but the words are empty and that strong I thought I had turns to dust on my tongue. I thought it was my truth that kept me fighting and strong, but holding tight to my truth is as stupid as Isa waiting for his abbi's bull to come save him. It is Miran that is my strong, and without him, my truth is nothing.

'Suck it up, princess. We aren't dead yet,' Isa says and puts his hand over my tattoo, stopping me from scratching the skin down to bone. 'Look, there's the moon. It's just like I drew it on the bricks.'

'It's nothing like you drew it on the bricks.'

Isa laughs like he thinks I'm joking. 'My ummi used to say that if you sleep in the moonlight, you'll go moon-blind crazy.' He smiles at me. 'Maybe we're moon-blind crazy now and don't even know it.' He looks at the moon again, his eyes wide. 'Do you think Miran will be looking at the moon too?' Isa's voice turns small and thin, his eyes held fast to that bright shining out at us.

'I don't know,' I tell him. I think of Miran's broken up body and pain filled eyes. 'Probably not.'

Isa doesn't make a sound, but I feel his tears falling on my leg and mixing with the rain. I think of Miran, the way he soothed Isa's aches, the way he poured out my dreams. But we're neither of us Miran.

I push Isa off my knee and pull myself up, not thinking of the pain tugging at my chest, just standing and feeling the rain thumping at my back and washing through me.

Isa won't look at me, won't move from the mud. I swallow the fear catching at my throat and reach my hand out to him. 'No use us sitting here wondering. We can't change a thing of what's happened, Isa. We let that fear sink its teeth in, we might as well roll over and die right now. If Miran isn't watching the moon right now, we'll tell him all about it later. Just like always.'

Isa nods, and wipes at his eyes with his sleeve. Then he's jumped to his feet, holding hard to my arm, and eyes set dead across the river. 'Esra!'

And there, just across the river, is a fox. Stuck in the shining from the moon, head low, beast ears flicking and tail all bushed and still. I've never seen an alive fox before, only the leftover fur and guts squashed into the roads. The fox blinks at us, then starts forward, stops again and watches, sniffing at the air and waiting to see how much harm we mean or how much meat we are. I can see his ribs beneath his fur, his skin twitching along his shoulders. One ear is torn half off and hangs in a scrap from his head. He tips his nose to the sky and calls a long screaming howl. Isa moves closer to me. The fox looks at us again, then he's gone, disappeared into the dark without even a speck of noise.

Isa pulls at my shirt, edging us closer to where the fox stood. I take his hand and let him lead me, my toes gripping the slime covered rock and sucking down mud, and my legs pushing against the river trying to tip us up and carry us under.

We climb the bank and Isa looks down at the fox's pawprints and he squats low, his hands covering the marks in the mud. He breathes in the smell of the mud and the rain, then he tips his head back and howls that fox's howl into the night, and the rain falls harder and harder with his howl and the wind blows stronger and spins circles around us.

When Isa turns back to me, his face is as bright and shining as that moon. 'I knew that fox was telling something. Look, a house.' He points to a cave hidden next to us, hollowed out in the bank under the roots of a tree. Grass hangs down like a curtain, hiding the cave and anything in it. I can see how Miran would be laughing with finding a cave like this. He'd be dancing and singing in the mud. He'd say it was the greatest house the world has ever seen.

'It's dry,' Isa says, his head all the way inside. 'We can wait here for Miran, can't we Esra?'

Isa's watching, waiting to see what I'll say.

'A house,' I tell Isa, and he smiles his smile up at me and takes my hand, pulling me through the grass and into the cave. There's a smell in here, of warm-wet and clay and fur. It's an alive smell and those walls curl around us, holding us still and safe.

My clothes peel free and join the grass curtain, letting the rain clean them through. I tell Isa to do the same, to let his clothes wash clean and dry out, but he won't. Just bunches up his sleeve and sticks it back in his mouth. Then he leans into me, the wet wool scratching at my skin, and I feel his heart beating just out of time with mine.

I take out my knife and scratch into the clay wall.
Isa and Esra and Miran

'This is our place now,' I tell Isa. 'And that there,' and I point to the scratched names, 'that's us. That's who we are. We exist. Now it's a truth.' I smile at him, and he smiles back. Then he takes my knife in his little hand and scratches at the wall under my words.

We folowd the fox and fownd owr hows

He gives me back the knife. 'Your turn.'

'I didn't think you could read or write.' My eyes search his, wondering at how many of my words he read in The Jungle.

'Miran was teaching me. He said everyone needs to know how to read and write. He said reading is how you discover your world, and writing is how you discover your self. It's your turn.' He points again at the cave wall.

I think a bit, then finish:

And the river will lead us home.

Isa runs his fingers along the words. 'With Miran?' he whispers. I nod.

With Miran.

Isa leans back into me and we watch the moon, shining up the water and the rocks and turning them white. On the other side of the river, a tree twists across the mouth of a drain, a black circle in the light of the moon. My eyes stare down into the dark of the drain, its tunnel pushing deep into the hill, leading far away from here. No one would find us in there. We've all heard stories of kids living in the drains, whole cities of them. Mole kids they're called. But they aren't

41

real, just the talk of all the kept kids who dream of running.

Someone's painted an eye, spiralled on the bricks above the drain, and it stares across the river at us. Isa is looking too. 'It's a giant's eye. Watching out for who goes past,' he says. 'Protecting all the mole kids. Can you tell a story about a giant?'

My head aches and I feel a rumble of anger build black behind my eyes. An anger that it is Isa I'm here with instead of Miran, that it is Isa I'm looking after, Isa whose head is so full of stories and the words of a crazy man that he doesn't even know he needs to be aching just as hard as me. 'Shut up and sleep. There's no such thing as giants and no such thing as mole kids. Look at all that water pissing out of the drain. You think anyone could live in there? If there were mole kids they'd be deader than the street rats.'

But that giant's eye stares out at me, holding me to answer for all I've done. I should never have left Miran. We should never have run. The Snakeskins always catch the ones that run. They find them, and when they're dragged back, they're broken past fixing and there's a dead in their eyes worse than any pain made by fists or belts or chains or boots. Not even a Whisperer good as Miran can bring those eyes back to hoping. That giant's eye has that kind of dead to it, and I see every eye from every kept kid I ever met, all those ones gone, all those ones lost or sold or moved on, all of them staring at me

42

from the dark, telling me they know what I am. Telling me they know that Orlando was right. '*You, my girl, are just like me.*'

Isa looks at me and touches my cheek with his finger, then he barks out a fox bark, loud and sharp, scaring all the eyes back until there isn't a single one left and he wraps his arms around me. 'I have a riddle for Miran. I can tell you first though.' He doesn't wait for me to tell him no. 'What's red and not there? You can give up if you want.'

I feel my eyes burn. 'I give up,' I whisper and I don't know if I'm talking about the riddle or not.

Isa's eyes are closed now, and when he talks his voice is hardly there. 'No tomato,' he says.

'That's as good as any of Miran's riddles,' I tell him, but his breathing has turned slow and even. He's deep asleep already, not even sucking at his sleeve. From far away, I hear the fox howl. I let my eyes close then, and the pain in my chest and head lullabies me to sleep, good as any song. Pain like that is like those drugs they put you to sleep with to break you in, the ones you can't wake from no matter how hard you try.

I sleep right through the whole rest of that night. Right through the sun's waking and the birds calling. Sleep all the way until my clothes are bone dry and stiff hanging on the grass. I'd probably have gone on sleeping all day if it wasn't for the whistling. My teta's song, whistled straight from the mouth of the moon and cutting through that pain drugged sleep to slap me wide awake. *Please let the moon that shines on me, shine on the ones I love . . .*

Isa is already sitting squat inside the cave, my clothes held in his lap, watching the whistler. I pull my knife free, the blade open, my fingers gripped tight to that knife twitching in my hand. I've never known a boss to whistle, but even still I hear a roar start inside my head. No one is taking us back.

I crouch down next to Isa. But the whistler is no boss. The whistler is no one. Just a boy, barely older than me I reckon. Isa's hand finds my shoulder but he doesn't take his eyes off the boy, watching him walking along the river, a too long scarf wrapped green and flapping in the hot wind, all bare feet and shoes in hand, his eyes pinched closed and arms stretched out and feeling for anything getting in the way.

The boy keeps walking, keeps whistling my teta's tune like it belongs to those lips, keeps on straight past us in our cave, past me with my silver sharp knife, and not even a bit aware of the roar sounding in my ears, not even thinking that we are watching and listening.

Not even knowing we are there.

Miran

Miran doesn't move. He isn't dead. That's what he keeps telling himself. 'I'm alive,' he whispers, his tongue thick and heavy against his teeth. And when his body starts shaking so hard that a tube comes loose, a siren and a wailing starts, and Miran hears himself scream. He keeps screaming, over and over until the policeman is holding him down, with something like a sorry in his eyes, and a nurse is pushing a sharp pain deep into his arm.

Then everything goes quiet. The nurse writes in his chart at the bottom of the bed and fiddles with the machine humming next to him. The policeman brushes the hair gently from Miran's forehead and smooths the stiffed white sheets around his body. Miran can hear the policeman shushing him gently under his breath.

'This room isn't properly set up for patients,' the nurse says sharply, stepping around the policeman to open a small window high on the wall. It reminds Miran of the window in the drying cupboard. Just big

enough to let in a little air and a little sun, but too high to see out of. Miran wonders what is out there, or who is out there, just the other side of the walls.

'The Overflow Rooms we call them,' the nurse continues. 'A bit of a joke, you see. This whole floor was a sacrificial floor, back when the city would flood before they diverted the river. This whole floor would flood, but it would save the rest of the building.'

Miran doesn't like the sound of the words. The Sacrificial Floor. It makes him think of rituals, and blood and dying, of people being sacrificed to the gods. Miran stopped believing in gods long ago.

The nurse keeps talking to the policeman, and Miran lets her words wash over him, and calm his thinking. 'These rooms would catch all the overflow of water, you see. That's what that great big open drain is doing in the middle of the floor, see it? Of course, when the hospital gets around to renovating, this will become the new Cancer ward and the drains will go. But for now, it's useful to have Overflow Rooms for when there's a shortage of beds upstairs. Although,' and the nurse peers at Miran over the top of her glasses, 'we've never used these rooms for children before. The doctor didn't say why the boy needs to be down here instead of the Children's Ward. I'm sure we could fit him in upstairs. I know that outbreak has caused mayhem up there, but this poor little lad all by himself in this room? It doesn't seem right if you ask me.'

46

'It's for his own safety.' The policeman turns to the nurse, talking quietly. 'There may be people wanting to take the boy. Children have gone missing from hospital wards before and we need to talk to this kid. We don't know yet who is responsible for what we found in that house – there was a group of them. But the sooner we talk to him—'

'No.' Now the doctor is in the room with them, looking over Miran's chart and listening to the beating of his heart. 'He is my patient. Now out. You are not to come in here again without my direct permission. I do not agree with police guards on children's rooms, and if it wasn't for the director giving us use of this particular room you wouldn't get near my patient. There is a chair for you outside this room. You can watch from there. Make sure no one hurts the boy any further. That is why you are here? To protect him, as you told the director? Unless you are in fact guarding the child or hoping to question him, in which case I want you gone. This is not a prison ward, Officer.'

'We need answers,' the policeman says, his finger jabbing at Miran, all softness now gone from his face. 'We're fighting a war on drugs, you know, and you didn't see my partner – this kid broke my partner's arm with a stick. He isn't all sweet and innocent.'

'I haven't seen your partner,' the doctor agrees. 'But that is irrelevant. This boy is my patient. He is a child, and he is ill. He is severely malnourished, shows signs of pesticide poisoning, and has extensive bruising and multiple broken bones, some quite old which have never healed properly. These more recent injuries are not at all consistent with your reports of a fall out of a tree either. Looks to me like the child has been hit with an instrument the same size and shape as your nightstick, Officer Watts. Now leave this room before I call security.'

The policeman looks at Miran. He opens his mouth to speak, his finger pointing again. 'I'm right outside. You try anything . . .' He doesn't bother to finish his sentence. He looks at the doctor again and turns from the room.

The doctor checks Miran's temperature and adjusts the machine by his bed. 'I won't let them talk to you,' she says to Miran then. 'Not until you're feeling better, so don't you worry about them. They aren't allowed to talk to you without my permission, do you understand? They aren't allowed. And no one can get to you down here. This floor requires a pass card. So you just concentrate on getting better. Everything will work itself out, you'll see,' and Miran nods and feels the tears swell in his eyes at the kindness in the doctor's voice.

They leave him alone then, the nurse promising to be back to check on him soon. Miran looks at the window, at the streams of sun catching dust clouds floating in the air. Esra told him once that dust was mostly dead skin, but for Miran, the floating specks make him think of the stars catching the sun to light up the dark. He watches each grain of dust, letting himself drift along with the specks.

It's home Miran thinks of, his brain scratching at remembering right through the pain and the medicine. He closes his eyes and thinks of his mother's face, wrinkled from smiles, and hair the colour of moonlight. He thinks of his pigeons, soft and warm, of his grandfather singing him stories, and of his sister's hands in his own, their laughing calling the birds in from the sky. His sisters would have grown so much. The youngest would be as old as Isa, she'd be seven. She was three when he last saw her. He wonders if she would even know him to look at now.

The pain is coming harder, a wave growing inside him. The nurse should be here to pump some more of the medicine inside him. To settle the pain down to a hum and make everything fade again.

Miran's thinking turns back to The Jungle. He wonders how much the police saw. Did they see the dead plants? The bat and the chains? Did they see the days scratched into the bricks, or the boxes of food left for them to eat? Did they find the pictures on the walls and Esra's words scratched deep, those words she spent hours scratching all about the room, her eyes wide and flashing, the rock cutting into her fingers, she scratched so hard. He wonders if they could smell the fear in that room, the same way Miran can smell the clean soaped smell of the hospital room, or if the police thought they had all chosen to do these jobs, chosen to live in this way. He wonders if they saw into the corner. But all the questions hurt, and the pain edges in then, and turns his mind to dark. And when a nurse comes into the room, a different nurse this time with bright red hair that reminds Miran of his cousin, he doesn't notice when she takes a phone from her pocket and lines up his face in the lens. He doesn't hear the click of a photo being taken. She looks at his chart a while and smooths out his sheets. 'The other nurse will be in shortly with your medicine,' she tells him, and Miran wonders vaguely why she doesn't give it to him herself. But the pain is pulling him deeper now. He feels himself fall into a heavy sleep, and he no longer knows if he's dead or not.

Skeet

Today is a whistler, that's for sure. Mam says I'm not ever to whistle. Says it cuts through her skull like an ice pick to the back of her brain. I tried it out just to see if she was telling the truth or exaggerating like she does, but this time I reckon she was being true 'cause she gave such a yell it right near blew me away. Then she sat down and bawled her silly bugger eyes out and told me '*it should've been you.*' I've heard that old line so many times now it doesn't even reach my ears. I whistled again just to get her to shut right back up and stop her wailing, then got out of there before the cup she was holding could find my head. She sure does get shirty does my mam.

But anyhow, Mam's not here and there's just a feeling in the air like something right good's about to happen and days like this are just crying out for a good whistle. That's what my dad would've said. He's the one taught me to whistle and all.

Course, that was before my brother got himself washed away in the river, and before my mam drove my dad so wild he decided he couldn't stand it a minute longer and went off to explore the wilds of Peru. He's gone there to find this plant that can cure just about any sickness in the whole of the world. He begged me to go with him, but I didn't 'cause of school. I might change my mind if I get too bored here or if Mam goes on too much though.

Anyhow, whistling helps me practise my sixth sense. Makes me feel good it does, and everyone knows you can't listen to your sixth sense if you're not feeling good. It's working too, 'cause here I've been, walking with my eyes closed all the way down this river for a good few minutes at least, and I've not tripped on a single bloody thing. I got the sixth sense from my Grandda Tom who used to know what was coming before it came. All except for his own dying which happened by way of a bus. The only one saw that coming was the bus driver and by then it was too late. I wasn't too sad to see him go. Apart from his sixth sense, Grandda Tom was a mean old codger anyhow. He used to twist my ears just for fun, and every time he saw Croakus he would try to stomp him even though he knew right well that Croakus is my pet toad and not some random thing hopped in from outside.

Croakus doesn't like me walking along with my eyes shut though. He's jumping around in my pocket and bellowing loud enough to wake the river spirits from their sleeping. My mam is right scared of the river. Says the river spirits took her boy from her and now his soul is locked deep under that water in the dark weed, tied up and choking on mud, and desperate to shake himself free. She's crazy as a loon my mam. There's no such thing as river spirits. My brother just drowned is all, plain and simple, and there's not a thing none of us can do about it.

Croakus keeps on his wriggling and bellowing and driving me mad with his moving all about. I know a lot about toads, that's why I'm writing a book on toad ownership, and I know that toads do tend to get anxious at times, but he's really overreacting in my opinion. 'I'm not about to fall over or nothing, Croakus. I've got my sixth sense, don't I?'

It was because I'd stopped whistling to calm Croakus that I tripped. Damn stupid toad messed it all up, and now I'm well and truly dripping. But if he hadn't, I would have walked all the way down the river with my eyes shut. If he hadn't, there's no way I would have seen the girl, watching me from her kinda cave thing in the bank, a knife in her hand and wearing nothing but a pair of jocks. She was probably going to stab me and steal my shoes and clothes and everything. That must've been what Croakus was on about. I'll definitely have to put that in my book. *Always listen to your toad. A bellow in warning sounds quite similar to a bellow of overreaction.*

My breath squeaks when I see the girl, but it's not

'cause I'm scared. Just 'cause I wasn't expecting her to be watching, all creepy like that. There's a little one with her too, I can't tell if it's a boy or a girl, but at least it's wearing clothes. Come to think of it, I'm not so sure the big one's a girl either, but her face is more girly than not.

I bet that girl or whatever doesn't know who she's messing with though. I might look all scrawny chicken, but I bet for sure she doesn't know what happened to Jeremy Jones when he tried to sneak up on me. I bet she doesn't even know about that fight club my cousin Sammy started last year, and how I won every fight I was in, right up until the very last one when they shut us down because some stupid boy went and got his arm broke. It wasn't even my fault. The fool fell over was all. Didn't stop me and Sammy getting the blame for it though. We had to camp out for days until Uncle Pete had stopped trying to swipe at us for getting him in deep with the coppers.

Croakus wriggles in my pocket, like he's getting ready to jump up and fight if needs be. Toads are loyal like that. Truth be told, toads generally aren't much good in a fight, but it'd be mean to tell him so.

That girl doesn't move. Like a statue she is, her fingers gripped so hard around that knife that her knuckles have turned white. It isn't such a big knife, but even still, knives don't have to be big to stab someone. And just 'cause she's a girl doesn't mean she's not tough or strong enough to stab someone. Mary from school is a girl, and we're all dead scared of her. She's just about beaten every one of us, she has. Course, when she went for me I wasn't expecting it, so it was hardly what you'd call a fair fight.

I can see why this girl'd be hiding out in a cave with a knife though. She's hiding from someone. Someone who doesn't like her much, that's for sure. Her whole body is covered in bruises. Bright red and blue and purple and green covering her shoulders and stomach like the bugger's gone and dipped her skin in a palette of paint. I've never seen someone look that beat before. But even so, how many times do you hear about a stabbing from someone in nothing but their jocks? Nah, I don't reckon she'd hurt a fly, this girl.

'Hiya.' I wave and give them both one of my famous smiles that light up the world, my dad would've said. It's a proven fact that it's much harder to stab someone who's just said hello, but the girl doesn't even nod, just takes hold of the little one and runs out of that cave and bolts straight into the trees.

'Friendliness never hurt no one!' I call out to her. But she doesn't stop, doesn't even slow down. I still get a good look at her though, stumbling up the bank and into the trees. Her back is just as beat up as her front, except it's got a whole spider web of scars going every which way as well. Someone must really have it in for that kid.

I think about following her, but then Croakus pokes

his legs out of my pocket and gives me the kind of look that says we've better things to do than chase dumb near naked girls with nothing but marbles for brains and poxy little knives into the woods. Things like turning back to town so we can get a pie from the bakery. Croakus loves pies.

I bet Croakus has forgotten we were barred from the bakery though – toads don't have the best of memories – and all because we didn't have the exact right amount of coins to pay for a pie. I was only off by a dollar, but the silly old cow still barred us. I would have paid her back later, but decided not to after she was so rude.

Croakus won't let up though, grunting in that way that means a pie is what his heart is set on, and if I was any kind of toad owner I'd get him a pie. I look again, just to make sure that girl hasn't come back, but the woods are still and quiet. Too still and quiet for my liking actually. Woods are meant to be noisy and busy, and I get that feeling crawling up the back of my neck, like I'm being watched by a little kid and a bruised up near naked girl holding a knife.

I run for a bit, just to get back to town more quickly. I run all the way back along the river and then cut up the hill and on to the path leading to town. But that girl and all of them scars on her back keeps niggling away at my thinking. I didn't want to see all that. Seems to me like something sort of private. That's the problem with eyes, you can't unsee a thing, no matter how hard you try.

That's what they told my mam when she wanted to see my brother after he drowned. They told her she would never unsee it, and that she should just make do with knowing he was found now and could be laid to rest. No one tells my mam what to do though, and she marched down there and looked for herself. Stubborn she is. Stupid too, 'cause they were right of course. She can't ever go back to thinking of my brother without seeing him all dead and puffed up like a blowfish now, no matter how hard she tries or how bladdered she gets. Maybe it's not the problem with eyes, maybe it's the problem with brains.

I'm so caught up in thinking about that girl that I don't even notice I've walked all the way to the bakery. It's the same silly cow behind the counter though. I might have a chance if I sneak in behind a fat man and just swipe a pie from the bench. That's what she'd think I'd do, so I might as well do it. Course, there are never any fat men around when you need them. Not even a fat woman, unless you count Miss Jinnie who's walking down the street now, but it wouldn't work with her. She lives a few doors down from our place and there's no way she would let me sneak in behind her. She might lend me some money for a pie though. She might even buy it for me and all, seeing as I'm barred.

Miss Jinnie's little one, Finn, smiles when he sets his eyes on me, and even though Miss Jinnie does her tight lipped smile that means she's not all that pleased to see me, Finn comes running up on his pudgy little legs and holds his arms out so I can swing him around in circles until he's dizzy.

'Skeet! Watch his arms! Skeet! He's too little to swing like that!' Miss Jinnie is flapping her hands at me, but Finn is laughing right loud, so he's clearly not hurting.

'He likes it, Miss Jinnie,' I tell her. She just takes Finn and puts him in his pushchair and says he's too little to play with in that way. I give him a hold of Croakus instead, and Miss Jinnie's mouth gets even tighter and she reaches into her bag for some wipes.

'Don't let those wipes touch Croakus,' I warn her, 'It's not good for his skin you know. Toads have real delicate skin, Miss Jinnie.'

Her eyes go all thin then to match her mouth and she mumbles something under her breath. I'm about to tell her that it's rude to mumble under your breath, and that Croakus is probably cleaner than she is, but I don't because I still wonder if she'll buy us a pie.

But all of a sudden I couldn't care less about a bleeding pie. 'Ho-ly crap!' My hands are in my pockets and I'm patting down every space I can think of, but they're not jingling the way a pocket should jingle if it's holding your mam's keys.

'Ho . . . ly . . . crap!' I say again, and then swear so loud that Miss Jinnie puts her hands over Finn's ears and tells me well off, but she would've done the same if she'd gone and lost her keys. It's not just the house key neither.

It's the car keys too that I took this morning so Mam wouldn't go out driving on her own. I really will have to set off for the wilds of Peru if I can't find those keys.

'Well dear, where was the last place you had them?' Miss Jinnie asks me.

'If I bloody well knew that, then the damned things wouldn't be lost, would they?' I try not to yell because I like Miss Jinnie, but *jeeeeez*! The brains of some people.

'Holy crap! Holy crap!' Finn says from his pushchair, all smiles and giggles he is. I don't think there's much hope of Miss Jinnie buying us a pie any more. Croakus grunts in the way toads do when they know they've been beat.

'That Finn of yours sure is a fast learner, Miss Jinnie,' I tell her, but she doesn't even say goodbye, just spins that pushchair around and stomps out of there, saying something or other about having a harsh word to my mam. Good luck to her, I say. If she can find a minute when Mam hasn't a skinful to drink then she's welcome to tell her any damned thing she likes.

I know just where those keys will be and all. There's only the one place they could be. Down the river where Croakus tripped me over, stupid toad. They must have fallen out of my pocket and into the water without me even noticing, and God help me if the buggers have washed away.

I run so fast back along that path, and even faster when I cut through the woods and down to the river,

59

it must have been near Olympic record time. And you'd think with the amount of rubbish catching in the river my keys would be caught up also. You'd think.

I'm not a crier. I haven't cried since I was in nappies, not even when I got hit so hard I needed six stitches, and not when Dad left, or when my brother drowned. But knowing what Mam'll do when she can't find those keys gets my eyes hotter than if I'd been staring at the sun. I'm kicking at the river, throwing clumps of leaves and mud and litter over the other side hoping they'll show up, when a hand drops down on my shoulder, like its straight out of one of those horror movies that come on after midnight.

That girl, she was damn lucky I was so caught up in key hunting, otherwise I might have taken off her whole arm scaring me like that. At least she's wearing clothes now.

'You dropped your keys,' she says, so quiet I almost can't catch a word of what she's saying. But she's holding my keys in her hand, dangling them right in front of my face, and that stupid knife of hers held in the other.

'Well what did you take them for?' I grab those keys back and check them over twice just to make sure she hasn't pulled any funny business. But that girl's face gets right angry then and she shakes her head just a little, then walks on back to the little one waiting in the trees, without even a goodbye or nothing.

'Marbles for brains,' I call after her, but not too loud.

She did find my keys after all.

There's something funny about that girl though, and that sixth sense of mine tells me I'll be seeing her again. For sure.

Esra

We wait. Isa doesn't take his eyes from the boy, and we watch from the trees until he is so far gone we can't even hear his whistling catching on the wind. Then we walk, slow and silent back to our cave, waiting for Miran to find us, just like he said he would.

We don't talk, just sit and suck in the day, trying to remember every bit, so we can tell Miran and make it his memory too. I'd forgotten all this. All the little bits. Like the white of the rabbits flashing their tails, and the way the birds chase the clouds and how the sun dances on the water. I'd forgotten how the river makes a kind of music when it washes over the rocks. I could sit here for ever I reckon.

But through all the watching and remembering my brain is burning, wondering if those police have locked Miran in their jail. If Orlando knows exactly where he is. Wondering if maybe Miran isn't coming to find us at all. If maybe we need to find Miran this time. Wondering how close the bosses are to tracking us down, and every walker that passes up high on the path across the river sets my heart thumping and my blood rushing. But none of them are Snakeskins. I can tell by the way they walk. Snakeskins stomp, hard and angry. These people don't stomp. It's like they have wings, the way they move. Like nothing in the world is pulling them down.

'Esra, I'm hungry.' Isa's hands are pushing hard into his stomach, but he's not complaining. He knows we can't risk going to find food. 'I know,' I tell him, and we crawl to the river and chew on more grass and suck in more water, fooling the holes in our stomachs to believing we're full.

Isa crawls back up the bank and starts singing to himself, the same songs he sang to the plants in The Jungle. I watch him piling sticks and old pieces of newspaper on to the mud. I wonder if he's making a bonfire to wish on. I wonder if he ever wished on a bonfire before, or if he was born too late, after all the celebrations and wishing had already stopped. He pokes about in the grass for a while, then smiles, picking at a lighter half buried in the mud. It only takes him a few goes to set that pile on fire. But those flames make me think of The Jungle, of Miran, of his broken up body and the way his leg and arm weren't moving right, and the sounds of the police taking him down. He seemed so small, Miran, who is bigger and stronger and braver than a thousand of those police. And Miran's eyes join all those other lost eyes. I should never have left him.

Isa uses his jumper to wipe the hot from my eyes, and I end up with more mud covering me than before. 'The day after my abbi died, he came back to me,' Isa says. 'After he was covered over by his blanket and cried on top of by everyone. Even after they'd took his body off to burn. He came back, his tongue all the way whole again, singing and dancing and not a speck of sickness on him either.' He smiles at me.

I don't smile back. He needs to stop believing in stories. 'Put the fire out. Someone will see it.'

He doesn't listen, talking on like I haven't said a damn thing. 'And later, in the camp, I was all alone, and every night trying to hide up inside of those trucks like the big kids. You know? The trucks that were going to the safe country. All you had to do was wait until they stopped and climb up on the back with no one seeing. I never could though. I wasn't fast enough. I was always too scared of the police. When they caught us sneaking on a truck, they'd hit us with their sticks and spray us with that stuff that burns your eyes and throat so you can't see or even breathe right. But then one night, before the trucks passed through, I was heating a can of beans in the fire, and I saw the shadow of my ummi, caught in the black smoke, and all the flames burning up around her. She was carrying my baby brother, and her other arm wrapped about my big sister and they were dancing more happy than I'd ever seen. That's how I knew they were all of them dead, without anyone being there to tell me so.'

I think of Isa, small and alone in those camps. He was never going to make it out. There are far too many wolves hunting in those camps. 'I would have gone with them,' Isa says, his voice just a whisper now. 'I would've walked straight into the fire and into Ummi's arms, but when I stood, the wind blew up and the smoke swirled, and their shadows weren't there anymore. They'd gone off dancing somewhere else.' Isa pushes his fists into his eyes.

'That's why I missed the trucks that night. Some other boys made it on, but they fell off after a bit and were smushed into the ground by all the other cars. But Esra' – Isa turns around and holds my face in his smoked black hands, holding my cheeks and looking at me, hard and sure – 'I'd see Miran if he was dead. He'd dance to me, no doubt. He'd dance and sing and whisper me all of his Tomorrow Stories and give me a riddle and tell me again about that bull that cried a river of tears, and there wouldn't be a speck of hurt on him either.' Isa puts his hands back in the smoke and starts up his singing again.

I stare at those flames and that smoke, trying to see what he sees, to feel what he feels. But there's just the heavy black of burning, sneaking in my nose and tightening my chest.

'The dead don't dance,' I tell him. 'That's just your heart crying out and fooling your head.' I dip my hands in the river, scooping up water and throwing it on to the fire until the flames are dead and Isa stops singing.

I leave Isa alone with the hissing of the sticks and crawl back into the cave. He stays out there whispering to himself, his eyes closed and his lips moving. I wonder how he learnt to believe like he does, with that fierceness. I wonder how long it will take for him to find out he's been fooling himself this whole time.

He doesn't say anything when he comes into the cave.

'We can't wait for Miran to find us,' I tell him.

'But Miran said—'

'I know what he said.' I take my knife and start to cut at my hair, pulling it off close to my head in chunks. 'He knows we'd follow the river. If he hasn't found us by tomorrow, then it's because he can't. We'll have to find him instead.'

Isa watches me for a bit, then takes the knife and starts sawing at the hair at the back of my head. 'You still look like you,' he says. 'It won't fool them.'

'It's something,' I tell him, and when I do his hair, he doesn't even complain when the knife nicks at his skin and makes him bleed. For a moment I'm stuck, just staring at the red drip running down the back of his neck, then I wipe it away with my finger and rub at his head to take away the hurt. 'Sorry Isa.' I wonder if he knows it's not the blood I'm talking about.

He shrugs. 'Tell me about home again. We didn't tell about home last night, but we have to, every night. That's the rule. Every night, after the second sprinkler-starts, we talk of home. Isn't that right, Esra?'

I stop cutting and lean back against the wall of the cave. 'Back home . . .' I start. But there is nothing there. Just broken words told so often there's no telling any more what's imagined and what's real. When Miran talks of home, he whispers my memories back like a taste on my tongue. When Miran talks, he whispers *me* back and I can feel the cold of the wind, and the sharp pull on my finger of the kite string catching and biting my skin. I can feel the heat from an oven full of bread and my mouth waters with waiting for that warmed soft dough. But I'm no Whisperer.

'There aren't any sprinklers here, Isa,' I tell him. Isa needs to grow up. We've no time for babies.

Isa just nods. 'Don't worry, Esra. When my bull comes, I'll make sure he sets you free too.' Then he lies on the floor, and I hear him whispering Miran's promise, word for word the same way Miran tells it. 'We're going home to the smell of the trees that whips in on the breeze before night. We're going home to hot cups of tea in the morning, and the beach and the sea warmed just right by the sun. We're going home to every one of our almost dreams that got whipped out from under us and scattered on the wind.' And he keeps whispering, until there is no sound and it is just his lips moving, and soon the slow of his breathing starts and he's sleeping again.

The knot tied tight in my shirt digs hard against my ribs. Miran would have told a story. Miran would have let Isa look in the smoke. Miran would have told anything that needed to be told, broken or not. But now all Isa has is me.

'Tears of a bull will set you free,' I whisper, and scratch with my knife into the wall above his head. Scratching muscled strong shoulders and a fierce horned head. In my brain, there's a picture of a bull, one I saw at a museum we went to when I was small. It was a picture from a cave, painted thousands of years ago when people were just learning to exist. That bull was huge and fierce with a quiet kind of power shining right from it. I draw tears falling from its eyes and turning to a river just like Miran told, and I wonder if it will keep Isa hoping. But my scratchings don't look anything like the picture in my head. They don't even look like a damn bull. I let the knife poke at my skin then, let the pain fill me, and I shake the shiver from my body and tell my eyes to follow Isa's and close, to sleep the rest of this day away. To be dulled.

The sounds of the river shuffle over me like when I was small enough to fall asleep to the hum of my parents talking into the night. I try to remember what that was like. I try to remember how it felt.

It's been a long time since I could really remember

my family. Not even Miran can whisper them back. I've only slips of images that are gone before I can catch them. I try to think of my ummi's laugh lighting up the dark, and the way my abbi would hold her in the kitchen and they'd dance to a music that only the two of them could hear. I know they did, I remember the doing, but I can't remember them, not even their faces, not even their voices. I think my ummi had black hair, long and curled. I think my abbi's was grey.

And instead of seeing my ummi and abbi dancing, my thinking turns to the only thing of them I do remember. Their bodies, empty and crushed and covered with the white dust of cement, the two of them still holding tight to each other under all those bricks. Like they were still dancing when the bomb hit. I remember my teta standing with us, the wall holding her up and the noise she made was an animal screaming. I remember the words I wrote on the wall above their bodies, later when no one was there except the dead.

They dance in death,
To their song, to their beat
While we wonder why we can't dance too.
They dance in death
While she holds the wall,
Keeping her standing, cracked feet on broken ground.
They dance in death,

While her black clothes turn white with dust,
All that is left of her child,
Of the place she once called home.

And then I try again to forget.

The air in the cave is thick and smoked. For a moment, I sit with my eyes closed tight, thinking that maybe I've entered Isa's dreaming somehow. That maybe this is how he sees and believes.

But I'm not sleeping, and still that smell teases at my nose, soaking in from outside the cave, a warm sweet that juices up my mouth and waters my eyes.

I edge from the cave and see him. That boy with his stupid green scarf and his too long arms and legs. He's sat on a rock just a little way down, his feet twisting at the mud and clouding up the river. But it's this boy that's brought that smell, and my eyes are holding tight to the bag lying behind him on the bank, full of hot roasted chicken and chips, piled high and steaming.

My throat aches from wanting those flavours on my tongue and that hot in my belly. A cold calm settles on my skin, and I think how hunger can turn a person to animal. I've seen it before. Two street rats fighting over half a sausage pulled from a bin, and the kid that won, he didn't even look back at the other kid, not moving on the ground and his blood turning the dirt to mud around him. That kid must have felt the cold calm on his skin too. It's what hunger does. And the hunger raging at me now whispers that this boy in his scarf is just a problem that needs fixing. It whispers that this boy would be easy to break, and my fingers close tight around a rock, the hard sharp of it pushing at my fingers. It won't take much, to get that chicken. I crawl forward, fox silent on my toes.

The boy starts whistling and leans down to the water, his arms stretching and reaching for something in the river. For a rock of his own. For a whole armful of rocks. I hear that roar loud in my ears and my arm swings high.

But the boy doesn't even turn. Just takes his armful of rocks and kicks his way down the river, leaving the bag of chicken. I don't move. I think of the fox and wonder if maybe this is a trap. That fox wouldn't fall for a trap. That's why he's not dead on the road or shot with a bullet through his head.

That's how Orlando did it. When He caught that girl, that runner. He lined us all up in a room, all of us silent and watching. All of us seeing her eyes, hearing her cries and smelling her fear. All of us feeling a fierce light, that it wasn't us kneeling on the ground. And the noise of the bullet won't ever stop echoing in our heads.

But my fox wouldn't fall for a trap. He'd watch and wait and make sure. I stay still. I watch, I wait, I make sure. The boy is throwing his rocks, making them jump across the water, and I hunch closer, slow and quiet.

And then the bag is in my hand and I'm back in the trees and grass and shadows, without that boy even turning.

The smell from the bag pulls at me and turns me blind. I push that chicken deep into my mouth, choking on the juice of the meat and trying to breathe through my nose so I can eat faster and quiet the aching of my gut. Nearly half that chicken is gone before I even taste the flavour of it on my tongue.

'I guess you were hungry, then,' and he's here that boy, standing in front of me with his eyes flashing, one hand on his hips and the other pointing a stick, sharp and angry straight at me. The chicken stabs whole and hot in my throat and I think of my knife back in the cave, of the rock dropped from my fingers when I grabbed the bag.

But this boy isn't getting the chicken back. What's left now is for Isa. I shake my head slow and there's no fear in the look I throw.

'You can't go around stealing someone else's hard earned chicken without even asking!' The boy's arm flies up and the wind of his stick brushes my face but there's a shake to his voice.

'Drop it.' And there's Isa, snuck up out of the shadows and grown taller than I've ever seen him, my knife held hard in his hand and pointing right at the boy.

The boy looks at me and back at Isa. 'What the hell? What is wrong with you bloody cave kids? I wasn't going to do nothing, I just wanted my bloody chicken!

What's wrong with that? Jeeez! You people!'

Isa doesn't move. Just keeps his eyes tight on the boy, not even a shake in his little hand.

'All right, all right, keep your shirt on. No need to get your knickers all in a knot.' He throws the stick to the ground, foot stamping the dirt and a hot anger all over his face. I curl my hand around the knife, and Isa grabs at the chicken, and now it's me standing knife ready, and Isa on the ground, hooked over that bag like it's the only thing in the world that exists.

'Can I at least have a chip?' the boy asks. Isa takes another bite of the chicken, then throws the boy a chip.

'I didn't mean just the one,' he says. 'Can't you share it out a bit? I'm hungry too, you know.'

Isa pushes his nose all the way inside the bag, breathing the smells and flavour deep inside him. 'OK.' Isa stands and leads the way down to the river. The boy looks at me with my knife pointing right at him, then follows Isa, turning every few seconds to make sure I'm not stepping closer. I growl, my lips pulled back to show my teeth, bared and sharp and ready as the blade.

Isa sits on a rock, his feet in the water and eyes closed. He's remembering. Just like I tell him to when Miran talks of home. The boy coughs and Isa opens his eyes. He looks at the boy, his eyes hard and not even blinking, and the boy steps back and pretends to be interested in a rock on the ground. Isa would make a good boss one day. He sniffs and holds the bag out to the boy. The boy's eyes scat to my hand and my knife, then he grabs at a handful of chips and jumps back away again.

'So what have you two been living on then? Rabbits and eels and wild pigs and the like? That's what I'd've been doing but I guess you have to be strong and clever enough to catch them, and maybe you two haven't had the practice like I've done. I could show you how, but, well, I guess there's no need now I've shared the chicken. And why are you two hiding out in here anyway? What did you do?'

Isa stares at the boy and pulls the bag back away from him.

'I didn't mean nothing by it!' The boy's eyes stretch wide. Then he reaches a hand into his pocket. But he's not quick enough this boy, and I'm standing over him, my knife sharp and ready, and Isa's on his feet with a rock held hard and high in his hand.

'Jeez, it's just my toad! Are you crazy?' The boy's hands are pushed in the air, and he's lying flat in the mud, a toad, fat and lumped in his fingers. Isa waits for me to step back, to give him a nod, and I wonder when he grew up.

He's not a baby any more, little Isa. Orlando would be pleased.

We don't talk. The boy sits with his toad on a rock, picking at the chips Isa gave him, his eyes jumping and wide. There's nearly nothing left of the chicken now.

74

I think again of my fox, of his ribs pushing through his skin. I wonder if he is watching, the smell of the chicken aching at his gut the same way it ached at me. I take the bones and the last bits of the chicken from the bag and throw them as far as I can into the thick wild.

The boy jumps to his feet when I throw the chicken, but then he looks at my knife and sits back down again.

'I'm thinking of starting a circus,' he says then, looking at Isa. 'A toad circus, what do you think? I could train them to do all sorts. Tight rope, trapeze, there could even be a magic show, and I could saw a toad in half.'

The toad jumps from the rock into the mudded up water. The boy smiles and pulls a bottle from his pocket. 'Oh, here. Raspberry lemonade, this is. The finest accompaniment to any meal.' He opens the bottle and drinks from it, then points it at the mouth of the drain, still dribbling its water into the river.

'They call that Giant's Drain. 'Cause of the eye and all. Those drains are like a whole other world under the city. They go for miles, running under the streets and between the houses, and there are rooms and castles and dungeons and the whole lot. There's even an underground river full to the brim with diamonds and rubies. I know, 'cause my cousin Sammy went down there last year with his mates from school. They didn't go that far in, mind, but on their way out they were stopped by this old woman who looked like she'd never seen the light of day. She said she'd show them the treasure, but they reckoned she just wanted to turn them into those mole kids that live under there. Sammy says the mole kids have been under there so long that their eyes see better in the dark than they do in the light.'

He looks at me then, pointing the bottle in my face.

'You've at least got to say something, you know. I'm not saying you have to yabber on and on like Great Aunty Mary does, or even be a great storyteller, although that would be preferable. Hell's bells, Croakus makes more conversation than you two do.'

He looks at us, waiting, his head nodding. I've not a thing to say, not to this boy.

Isa reaches for the boy's bottle and takes a sip. He closes his eyes and smiles.

'Is your toad a wild one?' Isa asks, the red of the drink dripping from his mouth.

'Hey? Croakus? He's my pet, isn't he?'

'Will he come back from the river?'

'Oh, he'll come back. He's just gone for a swim is all.'

'He won't come back if he thinks you're going to cut him in half.' Isa takes another sip from the bottle, then hands it to me.

The boy thinks on Isa's words for a bit, then calls into the water, 'It's just a magic trick, Croakus man. I wouldn't really saw you in half. And I'd put you back together again after. Jeez. Talk about soft.'

I smell the sweet pushing up from the bottle, and I

sip at the red that bubbles up and sticks to my fingers. It fizzes in my nose and tingles at my throat, and I close my eyes and think of the bubbles and the full, warm in my gut, and imagine it's Miran sitting with us instead of the strange boy who talks too much and too loud and too fast, and doesn't understand a thing of the world. But the boy starts up on his whistling again and my eyes stretch wide, watching that boy.

He's lying down in the mud again, his arms and legs snapping in and out, pushing the mud all up and down his sides.

'Aren't either of you going to ask what I'm doing?' He smiles again and there's something in his smile that gets my mouth smiling right back at him, just for a second.

'I'm making a river angel. Like a snow angel but made from river mud. It hardly ever snows here, and why should the Eskimos get all the fun, hey? Actually, I think you're meant to say "Inuit". I don't know, I've never met one. I don't think I have anyhow.' There's a sucking sound then as he pulls himself up, his hair sticking out from his head in clumps, and streaks on his face where he's wiped across with his hand. 'Huh. Will you look at that. It doesn't work so good. Too much clay in the mud. I guess we'll have to build it up like a sand castle then. Come on and help will you?' He grabs at Isa's hand, then looks at me with my knife for a moment before smiling and pulling at my arm. I bare my teeth at him again, but he isn't fooled. He must have seen the smile.

'Come on,' he says, piling mud up on the bank. The mud is all mixed with sludge and moss and twigs and leaves and he's turning it over and over and sending a dark smell of dead and rot thickening up the air.

'He will look more like a river man I think. Not a river angel. The wings just aren't working. Well, you know what they say about clay. You can't force it into something it's not. This clay knows what it wants to be and that sure as hell isn't an angel.' His finger taps at the ground and he looks hard at the pile of mud. Then he stands, his hands on his hips and his teeth chewing at his lip. 'We need something . . .' He looks around, at the rocks and the trees and the rubbish catching in the river. Then he points across the water, over near the drain.

There's a shopping trolley poking from the mud between the trees, like it's grown itself up from a seed. Something big and black is caught in the wheels, and the boy's walked over there, pushing and pulling at getting it free, talking on the whole time. The toad comes back and watches, his eyes blinking out of time with each other, and the foot of a frog poking from his mouth and still kicking. The toad looks at me and swallows the frog.

'Perfect!' The boy holds up a raincoat, waving it like a flag, and looking at me like he's waiting on me saying something. Like I care about a coat pulled from the mud.

'What a find!' he says, nodding at Isa this time. Isa looks away and the boy shakes his head again. 'Just you wait,' he says. 'You'll like it when it's done. Then you'll both wish you'd have helped.'

Isa leans his back into me, his fingers finding mine, and we watch the boy, laying the coat out next to the river and wiping all the mud from it, gentling it, and humming to himself like we're not even there. Then his hands are scooping mud and weed and sticks from the river and he's scooping faster and harder and there's an energy to it, pushing all that muck right up inside the coat, all the way into the sleeves, until mud hands spill from the ends. He pauses, and slows, then he stretches at the mud, shaping it into fingers, a fist, working on the arms inside the sleeves until muscles and joints start to push out from the fabric.

The boy starts on the chest then, smoothing, shaping, working at the mud, and his eyes go quiet and still, seeing something there in that mud, same way Isa sees in the smoke. And when he buttons the coat all the way to the top, the coat doesn't look just like a coat any more. It's got a living to it now, a breathing almost, pushing the chest up.

The boy looks at Isa, then at me watching, and he smiles, whistling bits from my teta's song, and pushing more mud into the coat's collar. His hands dip in and out of the river water, smoothing the mud into a head and neck, rubbing his hands over and over, the shape of it rising up from the ground. He works at the mud, turning it to cheekbones and a crooked over nose, a face growing out from under his fingers.

He reaches out for Isa's hand and pulls him forward. He stands behind Isa then, his fingers curled around Isa's own, and he guides Isa's hand on to the face, the two of them smoothing the mud into lips, turned down just a bit with thinking, same way that Isa's do. The boy smiles at Isa. 'There, you see? I knew you'd like it.' And Isa smiles back.

The boy rocks back on to his heels and leans to the side, his eyes taking in that half a person, grown up out of the riverbank. He stretches his hand into the water, and pulls up two round silver river rocks, shining with wet.

'There you are. Your eyes,' he says to the mud, and places them carefully down on the face. Isa hands him a piece of sludged up river moss for hair.

'Where's your knife?' The boy turns and flaps his hands at me. 'I'll give it back.'

Isa looks at me, waiting to see what I'll do, wanting that boy to keep on with his making, with his bringing that mud to some kind of living. I look at the river man and hand the knife to the boy, watching him carve and scratch, scooping more mud then smoothing it away, the blade knifing in and out until ears appear and a beard grows down in waves from his chin.

'What he could really do with is some trousers.' The boy hands me the knife and stares at me again. 'Well?'

'You can't have mine.' My head shakes, and his eyes go all thin and angry at me.

'Fine then, be a stick in the mud.' And he starts laughing like those words are funny. Isa giggles, then laughs, full and strong, his eyes bright and his face shining.

It's the first time I've heard Isa laugh like that. Like a real laugh, without a speck of fear or hurt in there at all. And all I can do is stare at this boy who can pull the happy from Isa and the smiles from my mouth, and who can steal songs from my memories and shoot them out his lips like they're his very own.

The boy finishes shaping a leg and looks up at me and laughs some more, his laugh bubbling out of him like the raspberry lemonade, and the sound and sweet of it fizzes in my throat and warms my gut.

'Hell's bells, I was only joking.'

He stands and circles around the river man. 'It's not all that bad.' He pulls a dead branch from the bank. 'Does he need two legs?' he asks Isa. Isa thinks on it, and nods, and the boy pushes the branch into the river man. 'Good enough. He can be a peg leg, can't he? Well? What do you reckon?'

'It's fantastic,' Isa says.

'Here, what's that in the mud? Dig it up, will you?' The boy points at my feet. 'Look,' he points again, jabbing his finger to get me to listen, to hurry.

I toe at a thin silver chain buried in the bank, and

covered around with mud and leaves washing against it.

'Esra?' Isa smiles at me and shrugs. I sit down on the ground, my fingers grabbing at the chain, but there's no grip to it, no way to pull at it. I wipe the sludge from the sides and work under it with my knife, pushing at it to lever it free.

The chain is cold and slimed in my hand, looped around, the ends of it burying deeper underground. I pull at the chain, and now I need to see where it leads, what it's hiding. There's a sucking, like the mud is fighting at keeping its secret safe and deep inside the bank, like it doesn't want to let it go. The wind picks up and chops at the river, the water rushing past now, fast and angry. I push my fingers along the chain, feeling them deeper into the wet. The mud aches at my nails, and I push harder until my fingers wrap tight around that cold hard buried deep. And when my hand pulls free, the wind calms, and the river slows and the sucking stops and all around goes still, watching and waiting.

'Is it a pocket watch? That's perfect that is! Good thing I've eagle eyes, hey? No one else would've seen that there in the mud. It might have been there for hundreds of years or more!' The boy reaches for the watch hanging from the chain. The glass on the front of the watch is smashed, the cogs rusted red and still.

The boy snaps his fingers at me. 'Give it here, will you?' But now my hands are like the mud, not wanting to pass that watch on. My abbi had a pocket watch like this.

I remember my brother taking it from my abbi's body, wiping it clean. I wonder what happened to that watch. I wonder what happened to this watch, how it got here, what sea it floated in on. And suddenly I'm back thinking of my brother, thinking of sitting in that black rubber boat waving to him, and my aunt and cousins following in the boat behind, those boats floating us away from the guns and bombs and killings and crashed down houses and crushed flat bodies. Away from my teta with her songs and her tea and her rug. My teta who wouldn't leave her home. Who was killed a day later by a soldier who thought she had her own bomb under her mourning dress. It wasn't a bomb. It was a book of photos.

We were floating to a new world, a new living. But not all those boats were made for the sea, or for carrying so many people. And when I turned to wave again, all I could see was the orange life vests floating in the water, and a hand, reaching out to me from between the waves.

Later, when we were walked up the dunes of the beach, I stopped at the top and watched all the bodies wash up on the sand with the jellyfish. I saw my brother, in his red shirt. I saw the men with their uniforms and their blue plastic gloves, coming to take the bodies away. I saw them lift my brother and put him in a bag.

I could never tell Miran that when he talked of us going home to the beach, of the waves and the sand in our toes, that all I could think on was my brother, dead with the jellyfish while those bodies washed up around him. I could never say, when we sewed those fake life vests for Orlando, that I was killing my brother and aunt and cousins with every one. And still I kept on sewing.

The cogs and wheels of the watch look back at me, like it's remembering too. I need Miran. I need him now to Whisper me back to hoping and dreaming and being. But he's not here, and I'm on the ground, aching and pushing the watch so hard on to my head I feel the glass biting into my skin, the blood running hot and setting loose everything I've been trying not to think, and I feel my heart crack with the hurt of it all.

Then the boy is there. His arm wrapping my shoulders, and his hand pushing my head to him. 'It's all right,' he says, and his body starts rocking us back and forth and he's singing my teta's song, his voice as beautiful and soft and river rich as hers. My eyes close and I'm small again, held in my teta's lap, back when all I knew was happy, and I can see her, as clear as day. I can remember.

I breathe in that moment of remembering, the boy's heart thumping at my back and the wind howling around us, and just for a moment I feel like nothing else in the world exists. Like we are the world. When I open my eyes, I'm stuck staring at the river man's face, and there's something about it. A kind of understanding.

'Well, where's that watch now?' the boy says. He stands up, and gives the watch a shake. 'Pity it doesn't still tick – that would really have been something, hey?

A ticking heart and all?' He doesn't wait for an answer, just opens the river man's coat and lets the chain swing the watch around in circles. I'm watching his face as it turns soft and his eyes lose their sharp, and then his mouth turns angry and hard and he punches his fist deep into the river man's chest. He stops, breathing deep and wiping the anger from his face, then he drops the watch down into the hole. 'Your heart and soul, good sir,' he says loudly to the mud. Then he turns to us and smiles, like he was never angry at all.

I look at the river man, his river rock eyes watching. Isa leans over the hole in the chest and spits on top of the watch. 'He's got your blood and my spit. He just needs something from you now,' he says to the boy. The boy smiles and laughs. 'Now you're getting into it!' He pulls some hair from his head and hands the hair to Isa. 'Go on then, chuck this on top and put his chest back together right, will you? You can't leave him like that.'

Isa looks at me. 'Come on Esra. Please.'

I crawl to the river man, staring into those river rock eyes. Isa pushes my fingers deep down into his chest. I try to feel what the boy felt, try to see what he saw.

My hands scoop at the mud spilled out from around his chest, my fingers running back and forth over the clay, cold and slimed with a living all its own, its form finding itself under my fingers, and I'm shaping and working the clay back to something of how it was, covering over the watch and the blood and the spit and

85

the hair, keeping that heart and soul safe.

Isa's hands join mine, and he's scooping and smoothing too, and then the boy is there, and it's all three of us making the river man whole again, our hands dipping in and out, our fingertips touching and urging, desperate to bring that mud some peace.

I keep on staring into those eyes, keep on searching. *Tomorrow*, I tell the river man, the words not leaving my lips. I think of the rain falling and the river growing. I think of the pull and push of the water, dragging up, higher and higher, that river running faster and harder, raging and roaring. I think of the water rising and the mud blooming, covering up and over the river man's body, burying him safe back in its bank, bringing him home. I hold my hand to the river man's chest, the boy's fingers resting on mine, and from deep down in the mud, my hand feels the smallest flick, pushing at my skin like a bubble exploding.

Tomorrow, the word echoes in my ear, in a voice thick and dark as mud.

The boy sharp eyes me. I close the raincoat, and button it, right to the very top.

'My name's Skeet,' the boy says then. 'What's yours?'

He's following us, Skeet. Right into the cave. And instead of listening to the river's music and the night sounds waking all around, all I can hear is Skeet's voice coming at us without a single let-up.

I don't know why I let him stay. I don't know why we told him our names. Tomorrow, we'll go. Without him.

'I reckon I might as well sleep here tonight,' Skeet says, 'with you cave kids.'

'We're not cave kids.' I push my back against the wall and watch for the fox.

'What did you say?'

'I said we're not cave kids.' I say it loud this time, right into those eyes of his, feeling that hard build again in my gut. This boy, this Skeet, he doesn't know a thing about me, about Isa or Miran, no matter how many songs he pulls from my head or how much happy he brings to Isa's eyes.

'I just figured,' Skeet shrugs, not hearing the ice in my voice. 'I didn't mean nothing by it, so no need to get all grouchy with me. You *are* a kid, and your home *is* a cave. So, I'm only saying . . .'

'It's not our home. It's—' I shake my head. This boy is nothing to us. I won't waste my words.

'That's good then. I didn't want to be rude or nothing, but it's not much of a home, is it? I mean, take the smell for instance. I reckon foxes have nested in here, and they're not the cleanest of animals are they? You live in this for long and soon you'll start to smell just as bad. Actually, if I'm going to be honest with you both, I'd tell you that you aren't far off neither. Maybe you want to think about taking a dip in the river or something.'

Isa lies down next to me, his head on my lap, his

fingers playing at the knot in my shirt. Skeet sighs loud and long, and makes himself a space next to me and the toad moves from his pocket to my knee, staring Isa in the eye and making him laugh.

'My dad sure would love it down here,' Skeet says. 'He's a right adventurer, he is. He's famous and all. Well, he will be when he gets back from Peru. Is that a drawing of a dog? There, on the wall? His ears aren't very good. They look more like horns. Did you draw that? I'm quite a good drawer, I could show you how to draw a proper dog if you want?'

He's looking at the picture of the bull. Isa squeezes my fingers.

'I know what you're going to ask,' Skeet says, leaning against me like we're friends. 'You're going to say "But what about your mam? Won't your mam be worried sick 'bout you not showing up at home?"' Skeet makes his voice go high and squeaky. My voice sounds nothing like that.

'But I'll tell you right now, I saw her this afternoon and she won't even notice I'm gone, the state she's in, so you needn't even bother with your question.'

'I wasn't going to.'

He looks at me then, trying to figure me out. He doesn't have a chance, this boy who doesn't know anything about anything.

'Oh,' he says and shrugs. 'Is that meant to be a poem?' He's pointing to the words Isa and I scratched in the wall. They're our words. Not this boy's. He shouldn't be reading them. I feel the anger hot behind my eyes.

'No offence, but it isn't very good. It doesn't even rhyme. And who is this Miran then? Is there another one of you cave kids? I've only seen the two of you. Is this Miran kid coming back then?'

'It's not a poem.'

'Oh, well then. 'Cause poems have got to rhyme. You did know that, right?'

I close my eyes and try to soften the hard twisting in my gut.

'It doesn't seem like you know much if you don't mind me saying.' He pulls his scarf off from around his chicken thin neck and scrunches it under his head. Then his eyes close and finally I can listen to the night's whispering closing around me and holding me tight.

The quiet is broken by a croak from the toad.

'I know,' Skeet says. 'That's what I told you before. She's got marbles for brains.'

Skeet's eyes are closed, so he can't see the look I'm throwing him. I look to Isa, but he's asleep already, his stomach pushed out fat by his full, and no doubt dreaming of clay and mud and smoke. There's the smallest twist of a smile on his lips, and I wonder which one of us put it there.

From outside I can hear a fox bark. I wonder if it's the same fox. I wonder if he found the chicken. I think of him eating, of that meat, fresh and whole in his belly.

I think of his ears twitching and feet padding soft and silent. And then he's there, in front of the cave, the chicken bones in his jaws like he's run himself, silent, straight from my thinking and into the night. He looks at me, his head down. He takes a step forward. I don't breathe, watching him close, my hand held out for him, my fingers aching at touching his fur, feeling the push of his breath. His head flies up. Then he's gone. My fox.

'Was that a fox? I knew I could smell fox in here. Damn pests they are. I'll bring my slingshot down next time and shoot the bugger for you, then he'll think twice before bothering you again.'

I don't say a thing, just wait until Skeet is properly asleep, his head resting on his scarf and dribble dripping from the corner of his mouth. I move Isa's head off my knee and open my knife. The moon is brighter and bigger even than last night, and I feel all those eyes finding me again in the dark.

The knife scratches its words into the clay above Skeet's head, and there's something in my thinking that says if I can get those words just right, if I can set them free, they might just take me with them. Even if it's just for a moment.

We are the eyes that turned from the fist,
We are the feet that ran from the rope, from the hunger, from the pain,

From the fear and the anger. From the empty promise of love and care.

I look again at Isa, at Skeet, and I hold the knife high to the moon, my knees pushing deeper into the clay and my arms stretched to the night. I think of the sharp of the blade cutting across skin, see it peel open muscle and spray blood, red and hot pouring on to the ground. I hear the scream of the dead before they know their life has even ended, and every one of those eyes in the dark turns away from the sharp of the blade.

We are the voices that whispered No.

I move back to the wall and pull Isa over me, my arms wrapping him tight. I look at Skeet again, his face burning into my brain. His toad opens an eye and stares straight back.

I won't tell him, this boy, this Skeet, that when he talked of his circus, filled with toads, it made me remember. That was my hoping, my almost dream, to join the circus. To stand in that tent, with all those people, held still and happy in just a small moment of believing. And hearing Skeet talk of his circus, I remembered the sound of those trumpets, I could feel the beat of each drum pumping my chest and my legs tingled at the pull of those tents. I won't tell Skeet that was the first thing I've remembered that Miran hasn't whispered up for me. I reach my hand to the wall and rub my words clean off. They won't be read by this boy.

I close my eyes then, and think hard on my fox, running in the night, of bushing up his tail, of letting the shadows disappear him. I let my thinking run with my fox, and feel that cool air pushing at our back, pushing us further into the night.

Miran

Miran wakes. A plate of food, covered and waiting, sits on the table next to his bed. He picks at the food, breaking the bread into tiny pieces so he doesn't need to chew. He doesn't eat much. His stomach feels full already, and eating is such an effort. But he does need to pee. He looks at his leg, his ankle held fast in plaster, and wonders if he has the energy to move on his own. The tubes taped into his veins are connected to a wheeled stand, and he uses this to pull his body out of the bed and steady him. It takes a long time to wheel to the bathroom. He sees the policewoman watching through the window in the door, her face blank. She doesn't offer to help and Miran is glad.

It is on the way back to bed that Miran's body simply stops. His legs weaken and collapse under him and he feels himself crumple to the ground. Through the door, Miran can see the policewoman back in her seat, flicking through a newspaper. He doesn't call for help.

He lies on the ground, waiting for his energy to come back. He hopes he can get back to bed before the nurse sees him. He doesn't like this feeling of helplessness, of needing other people to survive. He presses his cheek to the ground, and he concentrates on the feel of the floor against his body. The graininess. The mountain each tiny bump forms under his fingertips.

The vague light of the early morning sun shines through the window and moves gently across the floor, warming his feet and legs. It lights up a large metal grate covering a drain near his feet where the floor slopes gently downwards. This was the drain the nurse spoke of. The overflow drain. He imagines the city flooding, the water rising, higher and higher until the river simply carries him away. There is a quiet calm in that imagining, a relief.

A darkness covers the window, blocking the morning sun from glinting at the grate. Miran pulls himself to a sit, feels his energy slowly returning. He turns to the window. There is the silhouette of a bird, framed on the sill. Its head cocked, watching Miran. There is the scratch of claws and a trilled coo and Miran smiles, his lips stinging with the crack of skin. This is a sound from long ago. A sound of warmth and love.

The bird is a pigeon, just like Miran's ones back home, except this one is a dirty white with a flecked grey tail. Miran has always wished for a white pigeon. He stays still, not wanting to frighten the bird. After a while, the bird flutters from the window, cautiously, on to the table where Miran's food lay waiting. The pigeon keeps his eyes on Miran, pecking at the pieces of bread Miran was unable to stomach. Miran lets him eat, keeping still so as not to startle him, then softly, Miran coos, a tune long forgotten falling from his lips. The pigeon training song his grandfather taught him when he first learnt to keep pigeons. A song about riding the wind and following the rivers. A song of coming home.

The pigeon edges closer on the table, head tilting, curious. Miran keeps cooing his song. The pigeon moves closer, head bobbing with each step. Even from this distance, Miran can see that there is something different about the pigeon. His eyes are a bright, piercing blue, and peer deep into Miran's own. There is a knowing there, an understanding.

Miran whispers to the bird, all about his pigeons waiting at home in his rooftop loft, all about his family. He whispers memories of the living he had done, before, when life was still sweet and gentle. He whispers the promises he had told Esra, and saying them out loud again somehow breathes life back into the words. Miran's fingers move towards his shirt, reaching for the knot tied in the corner, promising to keep them together. But it isn't his shirt he is wearing any more, it is the hospital gown, and there isn't a single knot tied in it.

The bird looks again at Miran, then flies back to the open window, disappearing into the sun. A single white feather set loose from the pigeon floats down and lands on the metal grate, balancing above the dark beneath. Miran grabs at the feather before it can fall. He closes his eyes and breathes in the cold, musked air drifting up from the drain. He listens to the whispering of water from the dark below that crawls into his ears and shushes at his mind, and he imagines the river rising again. He thinks of Esra, of their promise to follow the river home.

Miran's fingers tear clumsily at the hospital gown until he holds a ripped scrap in his fingers. He ties a knot around the feather. 'Find Esra,' he whispers to the knot. 'Tell her to follow the river. Tell her to be free.' He lets the knot fall from his fingers through the grate. Miran imagines it catching in the storm water and washing into the rivers. He imagines Esra, following it all the way back to the sea, making her way home.

When the nurse with hair like his cousin comes in, Miran is still lying on the floor. 'What are you doing?' She asks him, but she doesn't wait for a response, just lifts him from the floor and steers him into his bed.

'It's time for your medicine,' she tells him, taking four large pills from a container in her pocket. She gets him a glass of water and waits while he swallows the pills. She doesn't write on his chart or feel for his pulse like the other nurse does. But Miran hardly notices. He is thinking of the white pigeon, of his pigeons back

home, of Esra, of rivers rising, and he closes his eyes and smiles.

Miran is already asleep when the nurse scratches at her wrist, pushing her cardigan high enough to hint at the tattoo inked black on her arm. The tattoo which matches Miran's own, of a snake curled around the letters O P.

'Sweet dreams,' the nurse whispers.

Outside his room, the policewoman continues to read the newspaper.

Skeet

That girl just doesn't make a bit of sense. I mean, there are much better places to camp out round here than this stinking old fox cave. Like the drains. They make for a much better place. And there's a big old entrance right across the river, just crying out to be explored.

Maybe she's scared of the dark though. Those drains do get dark. My mam's scared of the dark. Sleeps with a night-light on and everything. She's scared of lots of things, mind. Mostly she's scared of the water, so the drains would be extra bad for her. There's nothing in this whole wide world could drag my mam even close to those drains. It didn't used to be so bad, but now she won't so much as leave the house if it's raining. It's a miracle that woman even has a shower.

But scared of the dark or not, this Esra's not much company, holed up in her stinky cave and not telling me a thing about herself. I was expecting some stories at least, maybe a fire and some marshmallows, but she's no fun at all. And certainly not what I signed up for when I agreed to sleep the night, I'll tell you now.

She's too quiet, that's what it is. And angry. There's no need to be so angry, what with her poxy little knife swishing about the place trying to scare me. Last night she didn't say a single word more to me, which is just plain rude. The little one, Isa, isn't so bad, but he's only young so you can't expect much of interest to come out of his mouth. He hardly said nothing either, except to ask me if I had anything to do with bulls, and then to look all disappointed when I said I hated the things. Real strange them two are.

And neither of them was even here when I woke up this morning. I don't know why I even bothered spending the night with them and keeping them safe and giving them a bit of company, if they don't even hang around for a chat and a plan to get some breakfast.

Croakus and me feel like croissants today. Every toad owner should feed their toad croissants at least once a week. It's good for their immune system. I've put that in my book already. I know the best place to get them too. And if I can get Esra or Isa to come with me, those ladies at the cafe won't even think twice about handing some over for free, cooked fresh and still warm I bet. One thing going for Esra, is she's a face that'll turn those ladies' hearts to melted butter. Isa too 'cause he's so small and all.

I've just started doing some sit-ups, working on getting my six pack nice and hard, when the two of them come back into the cave, quick as anything they are and eyes wide as an owl's. Isa comes running right to me, and grabs at my hand to pull me up. But Esra, she's just holding her knife and backing herself in and under the grass, not even looking to see if I've woken yet. Plain rude.

'Finally. So where've you been? I was thinking croissants for breakfast. What do you say?'

Nothing. Not a single word from either one.

'You do know what croissants are, don't you? Because most people would jump to be offered croissants for breakfast.'

Isa keeps pulling at me, and Esra won't even shrug her shoulders to say she's heard my suggestion and is pondering on it. I've never in my whole bloody life met a girl that makes as little sense as this one.

Esra keeps stabbing that knife into the clay on the ground like she's not even knowing she's doing it, and her head keeps moving side to side like one of those dogs that rounds up the sheep. She's got her eye on something, and I can't help wondering what else that knife of hers has stabbed at. I wonder if maybe she took my wild pig suggestion to heart and has gone and stabbed herself one and now we're to skin it and clean it and eat it, because if I'm to be honest, I'd rather the croissants.

Isa pulls me all the way over to Esra. I move so Isa's in the middle. Not that I'm scared of Esra, it's just that I don't altogether trust her when she's holding that knife of hers. Made for a rotten night's sleep it did. Must've been why I had all of them weird dreams about river spirits and knives.

'Well, what's gone and got your knickers in a knot then?'

She looks at me, Esra does, with a real right scared written all over that face of hers, and without saying nothing, she just points that knife down to the river. I follow the point of the knife, all the way to the water. That's when I see it, what's freaked these two out so much. There's an old bum, lying dead as a doornail on the bank of the river.

'Hell's bells. That's real bad luck that is. We won't be able to drink a bit of water downstream from that now. Might be best if we find another place to camp out, further round maybe. At least until the coppers have come and disposed of the body.'

I look at Esra with the knife again and the scared and the big owl eyes and my back shivers with cold thinking what might just have happened.

'You didn't!' I gasp at the air and my heart starts pounding harder than ever. 'I mean, it wasn't you was it? That killed the old codger? You didn't, you know, knife the poor fella just to get at his shoes or something?' And I don't bloody believe I've gone and got myself caught up with a couple of cold-blooded murderers. Imagine that! Killing someone just for their shoes! The coppers'll probably accuse me and all and then I'll end up in the clink alongside the two of these marble brains. I knew they were up to no good. Didn't trust them for a second.

'We didn't touch him,' Isa says, and the little one's eyes have gone all scary again like they did when he pointed the knife at me, wanting that chicken.

Esra glares at me too, then turns back to the bum lying face down by the river, staring at it like she's not ever even seen a dead body before. Truth be told I haven't either, except if you count Uncle Jack which I don't because all we really got to see was the coffin. And Grandda Tom was too squished by the bus, so even though they scraped most of him up, I reckon there are still bits of him floating around, stuck to people's tyres and the soles of their shoes. But even still, you don't see me staring like that. It's not respectful of the dead.

'Are you sure? It wasn't you, now? Do you promise?'

Isa looks at me and spits on the ground by my feet. I'm guessing that's cave kid for a promise. I didn't really think they'd done it. Too soft, the pair of them.

'Well then. What are you staring at? Haven't you ever seen a dead body before?'

Esra turns back to me, and now she's glaring and angry again.

'He's not dead,' she says. And the way she says it gets that shiver running back down my spine even colder than before. And suddenly, I remember this bit from my dream, just a second of it, of all those river spirits

102

laughing and chasing me with their sharp little needle teeth and I have to rub the back of my neck to stop the shivers running all the way up the back of my skull.

'What do you mean he isn't dead? He looks right dead to me.' But I'm not so sure now, and he's too far away to make out if he's breathing or not.

'It's the river man,' Isa says. 'He's come to life with trousers and everything.'

I almost laugh then. I try to anyway, but that laugh goes and gets itself stuck halfway in my throat, so it comes out as more of a choke than a laugh. Croakus starts wriggling in my pocket, trying to get a good look at the body so he can make up his own mind.

'Don't be so stupid,' I tell Isa. 'Esra, tell him he's being stupid. Tell him how he's just letting his imagination run away with him, would you? Esra?'

But Esra looks at me and I don't believe it, but she thinks the same as Isa. Crazy, they are. Totally bonkers.

'Mud can't turn to real, Marble Brains. And anyway, we made our river man further down the bank. That there is just a dead old drunk who's gone and got himself washed up. Good thing he hasn't started stinking yet or we'd have to move for sure.'

I keep on talking, pretending like I know all about dead bodies, mostly because I sure as hell know more about dead bodies than Esra or Isa who don't know anything about much as far as I can see. But even as I'm talking, something in my head is niggling away at me. Thinking that maybe Marble Brains here might be onto something. Thinking maybe we *did* build our river man right about there. Thinking that maybe those river spirits I dreamt about all night had something to do with it.

'Look,' Isa says. 'Look at his raincoat. It's the same one—'

'But that doesn't mean a thing! Bums like that steal stuff all the time. Probably took it right off of our river man soon as he saw it then turned around and drank himself to death. Serves him right too, for stealing that coat.'

Esra shakes her head. 'Isa's right. It's him. Look at his leg.'

I follow Esra's pointed out knife and I swear to God in heaven my heart stops its beating for at least a minute. Because that dead old drunk washed up on our bank has a wooden leg. Sure as hell. Just like the one I gave our river man.

'It was the blood and spit and hair we put in him,' Isa says then, his voice all whispery quiet. 'That's what turned him real. Do you think? That's what did it?'

Esra doesn't say a word, just keeps stabbing at the ground with her knife. Then she turns and looks right at me. 'You made him too real,' and the way she says it doesn't sound at all like a compliment.

'He's not alive! Look, I'll prove it.' And I creep over

until I'm right down close to the body, me leading those other two cowards and the three of us sneak up real quiet, just in case I'm wrong and he is alive and he thinks to pull something funny.

That river man is face down, the clay all gathered up and smoothed out over and around him like he's been down there in that river bank forever, and the water is only now dragging him free.

But those two are right. He's alive. Even face down in the mud like he is, he's breathing good as me. I would've sworn on my dad's life that he was brown bread dead. But even being not dead like he seems, this fella sure does smell. It's wafting up from him like smoke at a barbeque. It's not just the smell of mud and clay either. I like the smell of mud and clay. But this smell is right awful, more a stink all mouldy and rotting, like seaweed and fish guts that's been sitting out in the sun too long. There's another smell too, under all that. A kind of sour smell. I can't rightly put my finger on what it is, but it's the kind that sends my nose hairs curling and my stomach turning.

'He smells of death,' Esra says, and looks right at me.

I nudge the river man towards the water with my foot, but he doesn't even twitch. Esra bends down, her face pushed right up close and peering at him, then gives him a real gentle poke with the tip of her knife. The river man still doesn't move. Not even a little.

So that's when I reckon enough is enough. I take a stick and try poking him harder. I guess maybe I poked just a little too hard, but I had to get him to feel it under all that padding of his jacket.

Well, that river man leaps up, slurping from the mud and leaving a hole in the ground, looking like a grave dug fresh for him. He's growling at us and biting at the air with his teeth all yellow and brown, and a bit too needle sharp and small for my liking, especially after all them dreams.

Esra legs it back to the trees, dragging Isa behind her, and the fool has gone and dropped her knife and all. I would have got the knife for her, except my hands were full trying to keep Croakus in my pocket. I would've preferred to sit down and get to know our river man, to have a chat and let him see that he's got us to thank for being alive, but I can't very well leave Esra and Isa, can I?

Riverman doesn't follow us. Just watches us run, then starts turning slow circles, his arms raised high and his face pointing straight at the sun, and jabbering away to himself. Growls and grunts and bird calls and kind of half wordy things all mashed in together. His head starts flicking backwards then like he's seeing things flying about and his arms start flicking all over like he's fighting off a whole horde of flies.

He's right bonkers he is. Wouldn't you know it? I bring a man to life and forget all about including a brain that will make sense of any damn thing. I suppose for a first go he's not too bad.

Riverman bends over the water then and I just about reckon he'll topple straight in and leave us to save him and all. But he doesn't. He stands, looking at himself in the water for a long time.

I guess you would want to know what you looked like, first time being alive and all. He doesn't seem too angry with what he sees, even though he has one of those great big hook noses like a witch from a fairy tale and his hair is all clumped up together and patchy. That was Isa's doing. He gave him the hair.

Then Riverman starts washing the mud from off of his face, and runs his hands across his beard and through his hair. That doesn't do much though because his hair is all matted, and full of mud and lice and fleas too no doubt. He doesn't seem to care though, and at least now he's calmed at bit. He reaches into the water and pulls out a stick. A nice big long one like a shepherd's staff, with a turned over bit at the top and everything. He holds it in his hand, testing it out, and then nods, right happy he is.

'I think he just found himself a walking stick,' I whisper, and maybe he's not so bonkers after all.

'You should've given him two legs,' Esra hisses back, but that's just not fair.

'How was I to know he'd up and turn all real on us? And I didn't see you making things better for him, Esra

Merkes. Hell's bells, you cried your eyes out into his very soul. No wonder he's as crazy as a loon.'

Esra must know I'm right too, because she doesn't say a thing back. At least that girl knows when she's beaten. That's something I guess.

I look at Riverman, my heart beating double time seeing what I've gone and managed to do, and thinking on how lovely it will be when I bring more and more people to life. I could start a whole village full of people if I put my mind to it. I could make little tiny people like elves, and fairies. And animals! I could make dragons and unicorns and animals no one's even thought of yet, like an alitoadamingo! I could start up a circus of them. People would pay thousands to get a look. I'll be famous! *Skeet's Miraculous Menagerie of Marvels!* I'll have to work on my methods a bit, but how hard can it be? First off I wouldn't ask these two for help – they're the ones that made him all loony for sure.

Riverman turns and starts poking about in the mud. That's when he sees Esra's knife on the ground. He picks it up, holding it a long time and twisting it around and around in his hand. He uses the knife to clean his fingernails for a bit, then holds it up to his ear, like he can hear it telling him all of its secrets. Then he turns real slow until he's staring right at us like he can see us in the shadows clear as day. He howls and his head flicks back a few times. He shouts something, louder this time and I get a cold chill all the way down my spine and right up the very back of my skull.

'What the hell did you drop that for? If he goes and kills someone now, it'll be on you,' I tell Esra, so she knows exactly whose fault it is if anything does go wrong. And she had a go about not giving him two legs! At least this way he won't be able to chase anyone down. I've probably saved a few lives there.

But Esra doesn't say a thing, just turns and sits on the ground, her hand on her head and her eyes closed, swaying just a bit like she's gone dizzy. Gee whiz she's a handful.

Riverman's turned back to the river, and he's looking over at the mouth of Giant's Drain, his arms held high in the air again. He howls again, then he walks his way slow and careful across the river, that staff of his keeping him balanced, and without even looking back at us, he climbs up the bank and steps into the drain. I said those drains were calling out to be explored. At least Riverman has sense enough to see that. And even though I'm right desperate to go chasing after him, to find out where our man is off to, and to make sure he doesn't get into any trouble, because really, we are kind of responsible for what he does now, aren't we? Even though there's a very small – almost not even there, it's so small – part of me that is just a little bit relieved that he's gone. Anyway, it would have been near impossible to get those other two to stand up and take responsibility for what they've done and come with me. Well, can't say I didn't try. I guess it's up to those mole kids now to look out for themselves. I've done my bit by slowing him down with the old peg leg. I bet he isn't really dangerous anyhow. Wouldn't harm a fly, I bet. He's probably just gone in that drain to try and get back to being part of the river again. Best thing for it probably. He was a bit too crazy for my liking.

'Well. That's that then. Should we try for another? Maybe a small one? A nicer one. We could make this one proper, as long as you don't go blubbering into it again, Esra Merkes. Esra? What do you think? Should we try again, now that one's buggered off?'

But Esra won't answer. And when I turn back I see why.

Esra's passed out, right there on the ground. Isa is standing over her, his tears splashing on Esra's head. It's a good thing for that girl that I learnt me some CPR off of one of those emergency shows. I've been wanting to practise on someone ever since I saw how it was done. Hell, if it wasn't for me, this girl would probably die right here in the dirt.

But she seems to be breathing OK, and there's something about her, lying there like that. Something so sad. I don't do anything then. Just pull little Isa on to my knee and give him a cuddle, and the two of us watch over Esra and see that she's OK. I remember to roll her over on her side so she doesn't swallow her own tongue, and then we just sit.

She doesn't take too long to wake up again, but even awake she isn't looking great. She keeps mumbling 'Miran' and I still don't know who this Miran fella is but he sure is important.

We help her back down the hill to our cave then, and she falls back asleep before her head has even touched the ground. I sit a while longer, staring across at Giant's Drain, wondering about our Riverman staggering through the dark. But he'll be long gone by now. We won't be seeing him again. And I didn't even get a chance to tell him who he rightly was neither.

'Well, are you happy with croissants then? Because all that excitement has made me hungry enough to eat a horse. How about you, Isa? Are you hungry?'

Isa nods, his hand rubbing circles on Esra's back.

'You wait here with Esra,' I tell him. 'I won't be gone long. Just down the café for some croissants is all. You'll be right, won't you? On your own with Esra like this?'

Isa nods but doesn't say anything.

'Croissants it is, then.'

I look back when I'm out of the cave, back at them two kids, all strange and no idea how to look after themselves. It's a good thing they've got me, that's for sure. They'll be right just for a bit on their own, though. I mean, really, there's nothing here to harm them now that Riverman's gone. They'll be safe as houses, I'm sure of it.

Miran

Miran wakes to the flutter of wings. The pigeon is back. He smiles and coos his song again, breaking off more bread and laying it on the palm of his hand. The bird turns its head to the side, but doesn't come any closer. 'Birds like stability,' his grandfather had taught him. 'When you are training them, they need predictability. They are learning to trust.' And Miran had learnt how to sit, still and silent, until the birds understood he could be trusted, that he was theirs.

As slowly as he can manage, Miran moves from the bed back on to the floor by the drain. He leaves the bread on the table, only taking a few small pieces with him. He sits as he had sat before, and waits.

The pigeon takes longer this time. But still it comes, flapping down from the window to peck at the bread left on the plate. Miran starts up his song again, and slowly extends his hand towards the pigeon, revealing the bread waiting on his palm. The pigeon coos, its eyes turned on Miran again, and slowly it edges forward, taking a step backwards every now and again as though it is not quite sure. It's beak brushes against Miran's palm, taking the bread and watching Miran, its blue eyes brilliant and bright.

The bird looks at him, waiting. 'I've no more bread,' Miran says. 'They'll bring more later. I'll save it for you, I promise.' The pigeon grunts, and Miran's grandfather's face flashes in his mind, his voice echoing. 'Why do you think the birds come back each night? For the seeds we throw them? For the shelter? Pah. It is for the stories, my boy. Stories sculpt the soul! Without stories, we are merely husks. Promise the birds another story, and they will always come back. Birds travel year after year, searching for the tales to shape their spirits, to set their souls soaring.' His grandfather pointed his finger to the sky, to the birds wheeling on the wind, making their way back to the loft. 'That is why birds are always free.' Miran thinks of the note his grandfather gave him, folded around a pigeon's feather and slipped into his pocket when they came to say goodbye: They can take everything from us, but they can never take our stories.

Miran stretches his hand slowly towards the bird. 'Come sit with me, and I will tell you the greatest story you have ever heard. If you wish . . .' The pigeon takes a step towards Miran, no longer afraid, and when its claws wrap his finger, happiness so strong it is almost a pain shoots up Miran's arm. Miran moves his hand towards his chest, nesting the bird against him. He had forgotten the peace that came from holding a bird close, the heavy fragility balanced in his palm, and the warmth from its body soaking quietly into his chest.

The pigeon coos again. Miran nods, his fingers feeling for the string bracelet wrapped around his wrist, and he breathes the first story his grandfather ever told him gently into the bird's ears. Of all the stories he had Whispered over the years, he had never Whispered this one. Not even to Isa. Not even to Esra. This was his. He feels now that he would like to have told Esra.

'In a time long forgotten, and in a place nobody knows, there lived a woman,' he begins, his grandfather's voice playing in his ears. 'The woman was as beautiful as morning, with a voice the colour of the sea and a heart as warm as the summer sun. She was a traveller, and walked many miles and to many towns, she met many people and saw many things. But one day she reached a town that the world had forgotten. The lakes had turned to dust, and the crops had long ago died. The animals had left, and the only people that remained were ones so bent by hardship and sadness that they couldn't bear the weight of living on their shoulders.

'The woman, who had seen so much, had never seen a sight as sad as this one. And so she sat right in the middle of the town square. And although no one was around to hear her, she lifted her voice into the sky and started to tell her tale. The wind picked

114

up her words and carried them over the buildings, past the clouds and beyond the sun, and scattered her words over the birds travelling past. One by one the birds spun in the sky, drinking in her words, following them back to the town, until, one by one, they came to land at her feet. More and more birds came, until the town square was a flurry of wings and beaks and claws. Birds of every colour and size gathered to hear the woman's tale. And slowly, one by one, the people of the town gathered, just as the birds had done. The woman swirled her stories and tales into the air as the rain began to fall and the lakes began to fill and the crops began to once again grow. She let her smile reach deep inside the townspeople, until they began to let go of their sadnesses. Then she gentlied the heaviest words from their hearts, until they remembered again how to hope. The townspeople turned to each other. They all had wonderful tales to tell, of golden birds and orange trees, of magical carpets and singing cats. And so they did. And from that day on, the town was full of birds and colour and life and happiness, and no one noticed when the traveller left.'

Miran keeps talking, echoing his grandfather as the tale grows and blossoms. He remembers his grandfather's smile, the softness of his hands and the scratch of his beard against his face. He thinks of Esra as he talks. Of Isa. Of all the other kept kids that he has told his stories to. Of the forgetting in their eyes as they listened, their minds flown into the tale, their souls massaged into something like peace, for just a moment. He talks and lets the words weave themselves into the bird's soul, in soft, fragile threads.

Miran lets the final words of the telling fall from his lips – 'I have another story for you, even better than this one. Come sit with me again, and I will tell you that tale, if you wish . . .' – and he yawns, pulling the air deep into his lungs. He finds that he is now lying down, his arm resting across the grate, and wonders at how the bird stayed so settled with his movement.

A sour rot of damp and mud and fungus clouds up from the dark of the drain below and hangs in the air. Miran thinks he should move back to his bed, but he is suddenly overcome by weariness. He feels his mind darkening and fading. He can no longer feel his body. He has the vague feeling that there is something there, beneath him in the drain. Something shuffling, sniffling, and listening. Something waiting. There is a soft growl and again the smell clouds up around Miran, but he is already gone, his mind no longer focused on its physical presence.

When a tapping starts from the depths below, rhythmic and sure, tapping out the same song he had cooed to the pigeon, his mind spins and he can feel that beat deep within his body, until he is the beat and he lets it carry him into the safety of sleep.

The pigeon does not move, and when fingers reach

up from the darkness beneath – thin, boned and black with dirt – the bird coos softly before taking flight. The nails on the fingers are long and yellow and starting to curl, and they reach for Miran's arm, grabbing at him, pulling hard until the grate marks his skin. The fingers find the woven black string encircling Miran's wrist. There is a glint of silver and a blade works at the string, nicking at Miran's skin and leaving a small bead of blood which dribbles into the drain when the string is cut free.

Miran does not wake. Nor does he wake when the nurse with the red hair enters the room, the tablets rattling in her pocket, cursing at the idiocy of the boy who continues to lie on the floor. She jabs at him until he stirs enough to be taken again back to bed, and he barely notices when she forces four more pills into his mouth, urging him to drink water to wash them down.

'Beautiful as morning . . .' Miran mumbles, 'Voice the colour of the sea . . .' Miran's eyes flutter briefly to see the nurse talking on her phone, and as if from a long way away, her voice, hard and cold, saying, 'It is done. It won't take long now. Thirty hours, forty hours maybe, but certainly no more.' The nurse scratches again at the tattoo on her wrist, and leaves Miran to fall back into a dreamless, heavy sleep.

Esra

There is a pain in my head, aching at me to stay asleep, dulled and alone, pulling at me to let go for just a little while longer. My ribs ache too, my whole body, burning with hurt. But pain is nothing. I've fought through worse pain before, and today, we find Miran. Too much time has been wasted already.

I think of Riverman, turned to living and rising up from the ground, his crazed talk, his jacket, his leg dragging, and the print of himself in the clay underneath. I think of my knife in his hand. I need that knife.

And just thinking of Riverman, his smell pushes soft into my nose, and the hairs on my arms rise and an iced chill trails at my back, warning of another person, here and watching. My eyes fly open and my gut tightens at the pain and fear, and Riverman leans over me, crazed and hard, that skin and hair all cracked from the mud, and those fingers with their claw sharp nails reaching at me, my knife held fierce between his teeth.

His teeth are like the teeth of dogs, sharp and

pointed. Like the teeth of my fox.

I try to pull back, to pull away but I'm not fast enough. He's got my shirt, his hand hard across my mouth, pressing into my gums, and I can taste his finger. Dirt and clay and blood. I want to fight and pull and run, but my body turns to rock, holding me down. Like he's sucking everything living right from me and filling my veins with mud as dark and thick as his own.

My face turns to stone and my eyes stop seeing and my ears stop hearing and inside I'm whispering my truth over and over. *I am Esra Merkes . . .*

He takes the knife from his teeth and waves it in the air, his eyes watching the invisible trails painted by the blade, his other hand still pressed hard against my mouth, holding me quiet. Riverman keeps talking in his messed up words and sounds and laughing and grunting. He looks at me then and his hand drops to my face, gentling the side of the blade against my cheek, watching to see what I do. I feel a prick of blood bloom and roll down my skin.

His river rock eyes keep rolling into his head and back at me, and there is something about those eyes, like they still have the river running right through them. And when he stares at me those eyes stare straight into my soul. He sees me. Sees who I really am, and I hear Orlando's voice playing again in my head. '*You, my girl, are just like me,*' and I wonder if Riverman hears the voice too. I don't turn away. And when he lifts his hand from my mouth, the smallest whisper of *Sorry* falls from my lips.

Riverman looks to the blood dripping my cheek, and his finger wipes it away, sniffing at the smell of it, lifting it to his tongue, and he tastes at my blood and smiles. He reaches into his pocket, his fingers searching, his eyes scatting back and forth. Then he nods, and when his fingers pull from his pocket a lump grows hard in my throat, and my breath comes out short and fast. His fingers, all dirt black and boned, are holding a black string bracelet that I've seen twisted around and around a thousand times a day. Miran's bracelet and no Miran to wear it.

Then Riverman swirls the knife through the air again. I think of Isa, looking in that smoke. '*If Miran was dead he'd dance to me.*' And without any smoke, without any seeing, I know stronger than anything I've known before – Miran's alive, and waiting, and Riverman knows where.

'Take me to him. To Miran,' and I point to the bracelet and touch my chest and hold Riverman's hand in my own, and his skin is soft and new. I put my other hand on his chest, and his eyes stretch wide to follow my fingers. He stills. And now he is smiling and his barks are bright and he points to the bracelet and then to the drain.

'Now. Take me now,' I tell him, and his head jerks

120

back and he growls soft in his throat, but he nods. I move to a sit and the dizziness comes from the black of my brain, flooding over me, turning my seeing to nothing but a dot of light holding Riverman's eyes in my own. I feel his hands catch the back of my head and he lowers me to the ground. He is whispering calm in my ear, and he sounds like the music of the river flowing over the rocks. His hand rests on my chest, just the way my hand rested on his, and I breathe the air deep into my lungs and close my eyes, sucking in as much strong as I can, because this is the beginning of our living, just like Miran said. Today we find Miran, and head home free.

There's a thump and a groan and the hand is gone from my chest. All the calm sucks away and my eyes stretch wide. Riverman is lying, humped on the floor. And there is Skeet. His foot on Riverman's back and a thick branch held tight in his hand. He smiles at me and holds the branch high.

Skeet

'Hell's bells, how many times am I going to have to save your life, girl?' Esra's staring at me like I'm the one just about to slit her damn throat. She doesn't even say thank you, just stares at me and then at Riverman, her mouth hanging open and her eyes all angry again. There's just no pleasing some people.

That girl is damn lucky I came back when I did, because I reckon she only had a good few seconds left in her. The way he was waving that knife over her head, he was aiming for her throat for sure. And her just lying there! 'Did he hypnotise you with his eyes or something?' I ask Esra, ''Cause I would have thought you had more fight in you, to be honest.'

Isa's crawled back from wherever he was exploring, and now he's looking at me with that same look Esra's throwing. He crawls over to Riverman, and starts touching at the skin of his face like he's intent on learning every little line and scratch on those cheeks. Then without even looking at me, he pushes my foot off

Riverman's back. I guess there's no danger in him waking anytime soon and attacking again. Not after the whack I gave him.

Esra looks at me again and crawls from the cave and down to the river, and now she's gulping in all that water rushing past, her whole head tipped into the water like she's trying to drown herself or something.

Isa and me follow, and Isa starts rubbing Esra's back again. He's a real sweetie he is. 'Well, I guess we need to work on our technique for bringing people to life,' I tell them. ''Cause I got to say, this one's a real doozy. I mean, what kind of creation goes around trying to kill the thing that brought him to life? Unless he didn't want to be alive. I didn't think about that. Maybe he was happier being mud and river water and rocks and branches, do you think? I don't know how to unmake things though. Hell, I don't even rightly know how to make them if I'm being honest with you.'

'He wasn't. Trying to kill me.' Esra stares at me, the water dripping off of her face. 'I was about to go with him – he was about to show me . . . He has Miran's bracelet. He's seen him. He knows where he is. He was going to – and then you—'

'Miran?' Isa asks, and a smile stretches across his little face. 'I told you, didn't I? I told you he wasn't dead.'

Esra nods at Isa and leans in close. 'And we'll find him. You and me. OK?'

I lean my face even closer. 'Yes we will, Isa. We'll

find him, for sure. But first, who the hell is Miran, hey? I've got to say, I can't help but get the feeling you two are holding out on me. Well?'

Esra tips her head into her hands and closes her eyes, just the way my mam does when I ask too many questions.

'Well?' I poke at her with my foot. 'This Miran fella?'

Esra doesn't say anything for a bit, just watches the river like her answers might just float past on the water.

'Please,' Isa whispers, and Esra looks right in his eyes and starts talking to him, even though it was me that asked first.

'When we were little ones, not much smaller than you, Miran and me, we schooled together back home. Miran sat a seat down from me in class. He was always clever. Always knew the right words. Always got the teachers to smile – even the ones who were grumpy and angry and told us we were lazy and had to work harder. Even they would turn soft for Miran. We walked the same way home and some days I would go with him to see his pigeons on his roof.' She stops talking then, looking all confused about something.

'I can't remember,' she says softly. 'Not properly. These are all just words and—' She hits her head with her hand. I'm about to tell her that she has to want to remember which is something I heard on a telly show once, but then Isa tells her to 'Keep telling' and she starts up again.

124

'Then everything changed,' she says, and she's talking so soft now I can't hardly hear. 'Little things, to start. School stopped, walking wasn't safe anymore. There was no more feasting. No more music. People started disappearing. Like they'd never even been. Never even existed. Us kids used to go and collect small bits from their houses. Just little things, like a pencil, or a card, a spoon, just something so we could remember they did exist, that they were real. We started scratching our names on the walls. Sometimes people wrote messages. One time I found a love song written on a door. And under the song there was a hand, just a hand, still holding tight to a pen and belonging to no one, like it had just . . . been dropped.'

And actually, I don't want to keep hearing any more. I've never liked stuff like this. Stuff like this just isn't right. Stuff like this is like a nightmare and I'm chewing the nails on my fingers and my leg is tapping and I wish I'd never asked and I wish she'd just stop talking now. 'You can stop,' I tell her. 'I don't need to know actually.'

'Then whole families would be gone.' Esra keeps on, like I haven't told her not to, and even Croakus has gone back into my pocket. Toads are real sensitive. They don't like stuff like this either.

'And I didn't see Miran again. I got on the boat and didn't see anyone I knew again. But then there he was, that night, in the truck. And seeing Miran in that dark was like finding my family again. He's my little bit of home. Letting me know that it did exist, that it was real.'

I don't look at her. I don't say anything. I don't know what to say.

'So there's our promise, Isa. Just like Miran told you. We're going home to—' Esra stops and takes a deep breath, like she's finding the words hard to get out. 'To build back our homes, Isa. And our towns and our streets and our schools and our parks and our playgrounds and gardens. We'll build it all back, no matter how crushed and stomped it's got. Home to the . . . to all of it. And we'll be so happy that when we are old and bent we won't even know when death comes to take us to the other side.'

Esra's voice has changed now, like she's reciting something in a play rather than really talking. I wonder if she's saying it just the way Miran does. She'd make a terrible actor if she is. I don't tell her. Advice like that can be given later.

'And the beaches,' Isa adds. 'Miran always tells of the beaches. And the sea warmed just right by the sun.'

Esra looks at little Isa and nods, but she doesn't say any more.

'I've never been to the beach,' I tell them then. 'Not even once. Dad said he'd take me down to the seaside for a holiday but he never got around to it. What's it like?'

Esra doesn't tell me a thing about the beach. Instead, she looks back at the cave, at Riverman's feet still lying there, not moving, and she looks so fierce at me I wonder if she's not about to attack me again. And now she's talking so fast she's tripping over her words and she's telling about a lady picking her out of the refugee camp, and how all the kids wanted to go, all of them kids on their own and no knowing where their families were and just trying to find somewhere safe to live. All them kids trying to find a home is all.

She spits every bit of her story at me, telling of all the work and jobs she's had to do, and how they were locked down in a basement until the day they found a way to escape but then their mate Miran got caught by the coppers and now they've got to rescue him from God knows where. I get the feeling that Esra isn't telling me all of everything 'cause she gives Isa a look when she tells of that basement and he gives her one back, but to be honest with you, I don't think I can handle any more. My brain's barely making sense of all this as it is.

She stops talking. 'Oh,' I say and use my scarf to wipe my face which has gone all hot and sweaty from the sun. 'All right then. So. Well.' I think for a bit, throwing rocks into the river to get my brain working right. 'And these Snakeskin fellas are after you and all? And there's no one you can go to for help?'

Esra laughs the kind of laugh people do when they don't think what you've said is funny. 'We aren't even allowed to be in this country. We're illegal. We're nothing. We don't even exist. And if we did tell someone? Orlando has His eyes and ears everywhere.'

She looks right at me then. 'Skeet. If they find us, we're dead. All of us. So go home. We're fine on our own. We just need to get Miran and go.'

I throw three big clumps of clay over my head and into the river for luck, then pull that girl to her feet. If she thinks I'm scared off that easily then she's dumber than I thought. What the hell does she think friends are for?

'Well then,' I tell her, 'If they're after you and your mate Miran, it looks like I'm just going to have to save you again, doesn't it? I mean, if you hang around for ever trying to get your dumb plan together, then that Miran of yours won't ever be saved, and eventually those Snakey-whatsits are going to find you all, aren't they? It's like in all them gangster films. They're after you, 'cause if they don't find you, everyone else will run for it, and it just wouldn't be good for business now, would it? You know, it's a damn good thing that you met me when my schedule is mostly clear, because usually I would be far too busy to be out running around with cave kids, looking for people and having to watch we don't get bludgeoned to death while we're at it. Well, come on then.'

Esra looks like she's doing all she can not to bury my head in the mud, but Isa is smiling again and I give him a wink.

'You're staying?' Esra asks, and her face looks more confused than Confusecius. Marbles for brains.

'Of course I am. Now get a damn move on will you? Time's wasting. We just need to wake Riverman and— Oh. Well. Would you look at that. That throws a spanner in the works now doesn't it?'

Esra comes to stand next to me, the two of us looking into the cave. The empty cave. Riverman is gone. Isa crawls on in, and is looking at something on the ground. 'Esra,' he waves us over. There's a bracelet been laid down in a spiral on the ground, and an oval has been carved deep into the dirt around the bracelet.

'It's the eye,' Isa says real quiet. 'That giant's eye. Look, the spirals are the same.' Isa points to the eye drawn over the drain, then back at the bracelet.

I smile and tap my feet. 'It's a sign, isn't it? He's telling us to go into the drains, that's what he's doing. Telling us that we'll find your Miran in them there drains. I knew it all along. I said, didn't I? Said we should explore all them drains.'

Esra nods, but there's something she's not saying, something worrying at her. She won't say nothing though, just picks up that bracelet and walks towards Giant's Drain. At least she's not soft. Not much anyhow.

Esra

The giant's eye stares me down. That drain, with its dark eating deep into the hill, spikes fear right through me. There's a sound, barely grazing over the water and rain. A washing and muttering like a thousand souls edging me to run.

'Can you hear that?' Isa asks. 'That whispering?'

'There's no whispering.' I tell him. 'Just your brain fooling you again.'

Isa doesn't say a word back, just stares into the dark, his face stoned over so I can't read a speck of what he's thinking. Isa doesn't know the promise I told myself the first morning we woke in the cave. The promise that said I wouldn't ever go back to living underground. That I would spend the rest of my life out in the sun and the moon and the wind, even if that life is no longer than a day. Because if I go back under, I don't know I have enough strong to get me back out again. It will strangle me. And I get it now, why the street rats don't care about belonging or being kept. They get to live in the sun and breathe in the air, every single day.

We've been staring at the drain the whole time Skeet's been gone, chewing at the croissants he pulled from his pocket, squashed and mushed but tasting just as amazing as he said they would. I won't tell him how tasting them makes everything lighter somehow.

Skeet wouldn't listen when I said we had to go now. Just flapped at me with his hands and said if we wanted to last more than an hour in those drains then we needed to go prepared. 'Wait here, I won't be long,' he said and ran off into the trees.

My fingers find Miran's bracelet knotted around my own wrist. I twist at the string, same way Miran did, and some of the fear pulling at my body and running my veins and crawling my skin is soothed, just a bit.

We hear Skeet coming before we see him. 'Supplies,' he yells at us. 'You always need to be prepared. I bet you didn't even think to find a torch to bring, did you? Or markers so we can leave our names to show how far we've gone? Damn good thing I'm with you, I'll tell you now. If it weren't for me, you'd have been lost and dead in a day.'

'We need to go now.' I step into the lip of the drain, not thinking about the shake in my legs and the way my breath is catching.

'Oh and here – shoes. I hope they're the size right. I had to guess and to be honest there weren't that many to choose from. We'll have to give them back later, but

131

they'll do for now. I grabbed them from a house not too far from here. They've loads of kids, they go to my school and all, and they're always taking their shoes off before they go inside. I imagine they've loads been stolen, what with leaving them on the porch like that. Probably won't even notice they're gone, but we should return them all the same. I got the torches and markers from them as well, and these – look, binoculars, they see for ages. We'll give it all back later. Well, maybe not the binoculars. I've never had binoculars and these are real grand, these are. They've this cubby house in a tree, full of stuff it is, just waiting to get nicked. Silly buggers. What do they think will happen? Still, lucky for us. It would have taken for ever otherwise. My house is too far to go there and back if we want to save your fella today. All the way over the other side of town it is.'

Skeet keeps talking. Isa is smiling, running his fingers along his shoes like treasure. I pull the shoes on to my feet. I can't remember the last time I wore shoes. I can't remember shoes ever feeling like this, like they're already part of my feet, soft and sure and ready. These are shoes for someone who is about to start living.

'Skeet.' He stops talking and looks at me. 'Thanks. For the shoes and—' I want to say for staying, but the words don't make it out, and Skeet is already shushing at me and telling me again how lucky we are to have someone who has a brain with more than just marbles in it.

'Now Isa, don't get mad, and you don't have to,' Skeet is fingering through his bag again, 'but I got you this dress. Different house it was. All their washing dry and waiting for some lazy bugger to take it in. But I wondered, just like, I was thinking, if the Snakeskins are out and about, they'll be looking for a girl and a little boy, not two girls right? So, well, I thought maybe, if you let me carry your jumper in my bag, and you could wear the dress and, well, I just thought.' Skeet lifts the dress from the bag. He doesn't know there is nothing in the world could make Isa take off that jumper of his.

Isa takes the dress in his hands. It's the same blue as his jumper and covered in small black birds. Isa laughs looking at it. He holds the dress up to his nose and breathes in its smell. 'Thanks Skeet,' and without another word he switches his jumper for the dress. Then he stands, his hands moving up and down the fabric, his new shoes jumping, and his face lit as bright as his fires with happiness.

Skeet nods. 'Good-o,' he says, and he's no idea what shoes and a dress mean to us. None at all.

'I've only the two torches, but they'll do,' Skeet hands me a torch, silver and heavy in my hand. 'Right, well, what are you waiting for? These drains, they lead all over. Mostly they lead into town. That's what my cousin said anyhow. But I bet you could find some that would lead you to the other side of the earth if you wanted.

God knows how we're to find Miran without Riverman to lead us. I bet he's left clues. Or maybe he's waiting in there. Or maybe . . .'

Skeet keeps talking and talking and steps into the drain, holding his hand out for Isa. We walk just a bit of the way into the drain, the sun still warm on our backs, and I turn and look out at the day. It seems further now, like a picture or a dream, the river and trees just waiting there for us.

I turn back to the dark. The smell of wet dust sneaks up my nose and sets fear whispering through to my bones, staring down the tunnel, with its black that gets heavier the further it goes. Like that tunnel has gathered up all the darkness of the world right here under the ground, and we're fool enough to walk straight into it.

Skeet puts his hand on my shoulder. I shake to get him off but he won't take notice, just grips it tighter instead. 'Do you know what my Dad used to say, Esra? He used to tell me that there's not time in this life to be scared. He said to breathe your fear right in and turn it wild and then you'll never be scared of nothing.'

'I'm not scared,' I tell him. Skeet still doesn't take his damn hand off my shoulder.

'Do you know what this drain reminds me of?' Isa says. 'The markets back home. The markets in the old lanes with the stone floors and the stone ceilings that curved over the whole laneway and kept out the hot and wet. Do you remember? The markets with the bread and the spices and the pots for cooking and the blankets full of stories. The shape of those lanes, it's just the same as this drain, only bigger. Remember?' And I stare at Isa and wonder if he can remember those markets – but they were crushed and gone before he was even born. 'I do remember, Esra, just like you told me to.'

I look into the dark and think on Isa's words. I think of Miran, of what Isa said, and of what Skeet said, this crazy boy in his green scarf who gives us shoes for living and brings mud to life. I close my eyes and breathe that fear deep inside me, and slowly that thousand strong whispering of voices hushes to the mumble of water tracing its way through the leaves at our feet.

'And, Esra,' Isa says, and there's no judging in his voice, just a desperate kind of hoping. 'Miran's down there, Esra. He's waiting.'

Miran

Miran wakes to a searing pain in his gut. He feels as if a burning hot knife is being stabbed deep into his stomach. And then he is vomiting, over and over again. He is vaguely aware of his body jerking, falling, hitting the ground, of an alarm sounding, of hands gripping and voices calling.

The policeman is in the room now, pushing at a red button and telling Miran that he'll be OK. He fetches a face washer from the bathroom, wiping Miran's face until there is nothing left in his gut to throw up, and when the face washer comes away, Miran sees that it is splattered in blood.

The nurse comes then, and another, and then the doctor, with the sharp in her eyes and the gentle in her voice. They clean him up and change his sheets, and all the while the doctor is looking over her notes and listening to Miran's heart and fiddling with the machine, her mouth frowning.

Miran's breathing is coming in short, fast gasps

and there is a heaviness to his chest. The doctor is pushing something up his nose now, and he has the vague sensation that he has soiled himself, but the pain is blinding and he doesn't care. Nothing matters any more.

Miran turns to the window, and he sees his bird, watching, his head bobbing up and down. As the doctor and the nurses continue to work around him, Miran feels his mind begin to slip, the blue piercing eyes of his bird enfolding him. He feels a great moving deep inside. He can see his white wings catching the sun, feel the warmth on his head. There are no words, just movements and great explosions of colour, pulsing and surging and twisting all the emotions of the world into a great kaleidoscope. He feels the soft green as his flock gathers around him and welcomes him home, the pure orange joy of coasting free on the wind, and the purple warmth of a wooden windowsill high up on a brick building. There is something inside that window. Something important, glowing red and warm as the setting sun. Then there is nothing.

Esra

Those rounded walls close me in, tighter and tighter. I keep turning that fear wild, just like Skeet said, letting it push me further and deeper underground. I try not to think about when we'll see the sun again, when there will be just a speck of light to promise at air. But Skeet's right. That fear isn't clawing now. It isn't dragging me back. Instead it's pushing me on, faster and further into the dark, burning my legs and fizzing my brain.

Our new shoes are wet and soaked, bubbling out water that squeaks and hisses with each step. And leading us deeper is a trail of hands, slapped in mud on the walls of the tunnels. Those handprints, just like the one slapped and burning with want on my chest. I'm following those handprints no matter how deep or far they drag us.

From Skeet's pocket, his toad croaks a long growl. 'Don't be so soft, Croakus,' Skeet says, his voice loud and echoed in the tunnel. 'I won't let you become a sewer toad. We're safe as houses down here.' The tunnel turns another corner and Skeet's voice starts up again, quieter now. 'Unless of course it storms. Then you'd drown, sure as a dog with no legs. Even you, Croakus. There's no escaping these drains when it rains. Now that is good poetry, that is. See how it rhymes, Esra? There's no escaping the *drains* when it *rains*. See?'

Skeet keeps talking about drains and the crocodiles and alligators and giant mutant rats that live down here under the city and all the explorers who went missing and were probably eaten alive.

'My cousin reckons there's heaps of treasure down here.' Skeet says. 'Heaps of people have tried to find it, that's why it'll be a right surprise if we don't stumble on at least a few skeletons. If we're lucky, we might even find the treasure! What do you reckon? We could be richer and famouser than anyone!'

We keep following those prints, the tunnels twisting and turning, faster and further, growing then shrinking, squashing down smaller; the ceiling getting lower and the sides squeezing tight so we're forced to our hands and knees, spiders' webs sticking to our faces, pushing through the sludge and rubbish and waking the smell of dead and rot. A half-eaten rat squashes between my leg and the wall, its eyes black and open, staring right at me. I feel its fur on my skin, wet and slimed and we push further, each step dragging us closer to the belly of the earth, waiting for Riverman to melt from the shadows and bring us to Miran.

The ceiling rises again and we follow the handprints, past waterfalls crashing water to the drains lower down, and ladders leading to more and more tunnels. We keep going, past the nests of rats and birds, and through rooms with blades of rock that hang from the ceilings above us. We go past numbered doors set so high up the walls you'd need wings to get up there, and every now and then, we catch just a snip of sound. Some music, or laughing, or the sound from far off of a baby crying.

'Mole kids,' Isa whispers, and his face is filled with light.

We follow the drain around a bend, and now we're close. The smell of wet animal hangs harder in the air, Riverman's smell. Skeet's fingers grip my hand again, and this time I don't shake him off. This time my hand grabs at his arm and grips right back.

Skeet is the one who sees it first. His torch catches just the finest scrap of green breaking through the red bricks of the drain wall. We stop and shine our torches along the green, following the trail with our light. It's a picture, right there on the wall, all pieced together with bits of broken glass and shards of metal. There's a realness to it, like a whole world has been planted down here, just waiting to grow up and out of those bricks. It feels to me like if we knew how, we could step straight from this drain and into that world and never have to look back.

The green glass turns to ocean, spilling out into the drain as though all the water we've been stepping through has streamed right from this picture and into our world. A rocked mountain towers up over the top of the sea, a bird's nest sheltered in between the rocks, and just a piece of the sun shining through the grey of the sky. And there is the handprint burning bright from the top of the picture, calling us closer.

'Esra,' Isa says, standing up on the tops of his toes and dancing around trying to take in the whole of the picture. 'It's home, isn't it?' he says, a wonder grown on his face. 'Just like Miran told it. There's the sea where we'll swim and the mountains to explore and the trees to climb, and the sun that will warm at our backs. It's home just like it was before, isn't it, Esra? Just like it will be again. Esra? Is this home?'

I look again at the picture. It is home. The home I've forgotten. The home Miran's talked of in his Tomorrow Stories, jumped straight from his lips into the dark and come to life on the wall of an underground drain. *With our souls tied together, we won't ever be apart.*

Skeet moves towards the picture. He's looking at the broken glass bird's nest, two small white eggs catching at the torch light, his finger edging the nest. 'Esra, look—' He pulls at me. It's just like the rest of the picture, made of glass and bottle tops. All except for one, small egg. It's a shell, a real eggshell, cracked open and empty, nested against that wall by the glass. A small yellow feather has caught and washes in and out with our breathing.

'There's Miran's pigeon,' Isa points to the picture where a bone white bird turns circles in the air.

'Miran says they do that for fun,' I tell Isa. Skeet looks at me with eyebrows raised and I turn back to Isa. 'See how it's almost upside down? They do that when they fly, just for fun. Did Miran tell you about his pigeons? He races them. He'll give you a baby, so you can raise it and grow it up.' And looking at that picture and telling Isa, it's like Miran is right there next to me, talking all about his birds, his hands working the air in front of him. 'They're smart, Isa, and can even read the alphabet. And they remember people's faces, so your bird will never forget you, no matter where on this earth you are, she'll know you. And they're brave, Isa, the bravest of birds—'

'Pigeons are nothing but rats of the sky,' Skeet's voice crashes over my own. 'If you're going to keep a bird, you should keep a nice one at least. A swan or a parrot or a toucan or something. A flamingo even, they're nice. But a pigeon? No way. Filthy and dumb as a dodo, they are. Hell, they eat rubbish and live in their own crap. And don't believe anyone who tells you that being crapped on by a pigeon is good luck. It's not. I've been crapped on and didn't get any luck at all, so I know.' Skeet takes another look at the picture and sniffs. 'Stupidest bird there is if you ask me. Well, come on then. We've not got all day you know.'

Skeet turns, his torch flashing down the tunnel, and

the light of it catches on a speck of white, the hint of moving in the dark. I hear Skeet's breath suck in sharp and he steps back against me and I feel the shiver in his arms. Slowly, he lets the light sweep back again, searching for the glint, for who we know is there, watching us from the shadows.

The torch lights up his foot, his twisted toes curled like claws, and there's Riverman, crouched and hiding in the dark. I feel my heart bursting with the nearness of finding Miran, of running free, of getting home. *And then our living will start.* My hand is squeezing Isa's shoulder, letting him know that our Tomorrow is now. That this is it, our waiting is done, we are free and we will never be kept again. That dream is so close now I can just about feel the hot of bread in my mouth.

Skeet keeps his torch held tight on Riverman, lighting up his sharpened teeth, snapping and snarled. There's something about him down in these drains that wasn't there before. A raw wild, and when I take a step towards him, Riverman pulls his shoulders up towards his head, dog angry, a low growl rumbling from his chest.

He pulls himself up on the wall, his words blurring with the whisper of the water trickling by our feet, and there isn't even a hint of smile in his look. Instead, there's an anger there, beast wild and fierce, and a chill eats at my neck, wondering if maybe we took too long.

Skeet pulls on my arm. 'Esra,' he says, and now I can hear the fear catching his voice.

143

Riverman takes a step towards us, then stops. He tips his head to the side, listening. Then he opens his mouth and starts to laugh. He laughs, louder and louder until the sound is bouncing around the drains and forcing us back. There's no beauty to his laugh now. Just a hard cold. But we are so close to Miran, to home, to free.

'Where is he? Take me to him. Miran?' And I am twisting Miran's bracelet in my fingers so he sees and pointing to the picture, to Miran's story there on the wall. But Riverman just keeps laughing. His eyes are burning now and there is no comfort, no understanding at all. He looks at me once, his tongue darting out between his teeth, then he turns into the dark and disappears. And the promise of today being the start of our living turns to dust.

Miran

When Miran wakes, he finds himself on the floor again, near the grate. He has no memory of moving himself there, but the wheeled stand is next to him, upright and dripping fluid gently into his body. There is the smell again, smoking up from the drain, stronger now than it had been before, and when it curls over him, Miran feels as if he is being dragged under the ground. That's what it smells like. The wet dark of earth so deep that the sun hasn't ever licked at it.

Miran takes a deep breath. He remembers the incredible pain from before, but there is only a small shadow of that now. His stomach is tender, and although his body aches with tiredness, his mind is slowly waking, shaking off the thick fog where memory should have been. A riddle comes to him then, and he smiles. What is as light as a feather, but not even the strongest person on earth can hold it for more than a few minutes? He wonders if he has already told Esra this one, and thinks of the scowl she would give him.

She always says she hates his riddles. She always tries to answer them though.

There is a soft hiss from the drain below, and when Miran peers into the grate, he imagines that there is a heaviness to the dark that wasn't there before, as though there is something waiting and watching from in the drain. He vaguely remembers feeling this before, he thinks he had heard noises last time, growls and snorts, but his memory is blurred and unsure, flashes of dreams and stories mingling with the voices of nurses and doctors and beeping, angry machines. His fingers tear again at the hospital gown, and he knots the fabric and whispers into it. 'Find Esra,' he says, and lets the knot drop into the drain. He hears a shuffle and peers again into the dark, a flicker of fear playing at the back of his neck.

There is a slapping of wings and Miran looks to the window. There he is, his bird, keeping watch from the sill. Miran's hand lifts towards the bird and the bird falls on to Miran's outstretched finger. 'You came back,' he whispers. 'For another story?' And his fingers move to his wrist, to twist at the black string as he always does. But his bracelet is gone and Miran feels the panic rise up in his gut. His mother had woven that bracelet, whispering his future into its string. 'This will keep you safe. It will bring you home to me,' his mother had told him as she tied the knot around his wrist.

And suddenly Miran is back in the tent in the field,

his sisters around him, tugging at his fingers, holding tight to his waist. There is his mother. Smiling, with tears falling down her cheeks. The man stands behind Miran, waiting to take him away, to put him in the truck.

The man hands over an envelope. 'This is just a small part of the money Miran will be making. A down payment so you can meet this month's rent. I know how much they charge for tents in this field. This is nothing compared to what Miran will be earning – even after we take some for his school and board. Where we are taking him, the pay is very good.'

The man's hand is heavy on Miran's shoulder, and Miran feels a confused sense of fear and pride. 'The harder he works,' the man continues, 'the more money you will receive, Ma'am. It's good, soft work too – not tiring like the potato picking and brick carrying he must do here. Where we are going, children aren't allowed to work so hard. He will only work weekends so he can concentrate on his studies. But where we are going they pay many dollars for just a few hours work. And with the money he sends back, you will be able to eat three meals a day, instead of just one. Then you won't need to worry about your daughters so much. You won't need to marry them off so young. Twelve is still so young to be married.' The man looks at Miran's oldest sister. She had already had one offer of marriage. 'Or perhaps it is one of the girls who needs an education most?'

Miran's mother shakes her head. 'Miran is the

cleverest,' she says. 'He will do well with schooling,' and the man smiles and agrees. 'Miran it is then.'

And then the memory is gone, and Miran finds himself back in the hospital room, staring into the dark of the drain. He tells himself that the nurse must have cut the bracelet, to make space for the tube that is taped to his arm. He will get it back, next time she comes.

The bird swells his throat, grunting, his head bowing and feathers fluffed, and Miran realises he has been holding the bird too hard. He lowers his mouth to the bird, his lips gently kissing the soft feathers. 'I am sorry, little one. So then, a story.' And Miran closes his eyes and begins.

'In a time long forgotten, in a place nobody knows . . .'

Miran listens to his grandfather's voice playing in his memory, and as he talks, Miran thinks of home. He thinks of the days spent playing, he thinks of his family before they had to leave. Of his mother's kiss as she left for work, of walking with his grandfather to the library. He thinks of the smell of the library, that musked smell of paper promising a million new worlds to discover and an infinity of existences to explore. He thinks of his father, cooking the meal at night, and the laughter of a family come together to eat.

Miran keeps telling his story, and with each word that drops from his lips, he sees his family, remembers a small detail long forgotten. By the time the story has come to an end, Miran is covered with the soft glow of being with those you love.

When he is done, he whispers to the bird, 'I have another story for you, even greater than this one. Come sit with me again, and I will tell you that tale, if you wish . . .' He lifts his hand and the bird trills softly before flying to the window. It stops and turns, cocking its head to the side, then flies free.

Miran pulls himself to a stand and stumbles back into his bed. When the nurse arrives soon after with a tray, she beams down at him. 'So you're awake!' she says and claps her hands together. 'It looks as though you're feeling much better then?' Miran nods and allows the nurse to help him into a sit.

'Are you hungry at all? This jelly is good for a sore tummy. Or I can get you an icy-pole if you prefer?'

'I was wearing a bracelet,' Miran says. 'A string bracelet. I need it back.' The nurse stops for a moment and looks at Miran's wrist. 'Yes lovey, I remember. It was a beauty. The black one, right? I didn't take it, love. There was no need.'

'Maybe the other nurse did? The one with red hair?'

But the nurse just looks puzzled and shakes her head. 'There's not a nurse I know working this floor with hair like that. But I'll ask around for you, pet. I'm sure it'll turn up.'

Sleep falls heavily on Miran. He doesn't dream. He simply becomes still, his mind black. He wakes when *the doctor checks on him, and she too smiles and says how much better he is doing, that he seemed to be allergic to some of the medicine he's had, but they'd sorted it now. He wants to ask her about his bracelet, to tell her he needs it, but he is so, so tired again.*

Miran doesn't hear the rain begin to fall outside, or the thunder begin to rumble, getting closer. He sleeps, soundly and heavily, as all around him, the rain comes falling down.

Esra

We follow Riverman into the dark. I grab Isa's hand in mine and we splash after him, our hands running along the walls steadying us from falling, our torches flicking shadows around us. I wonder then how Riverman sees in this dark, with nothing to light his way.

He's dodging our light, keeping to the shadows, but we can hear him, his wooden leg dragging through the drains, his grunts and wheezing in and out, and that laugh of his, softer now but just as wild.

This drain has no turns, no side tunnels breaking off and winding around. This is just one long burrow of darkness. Riverman goes faster and faster until the dark has swallowed him whole and it's only the noise of our own footsteps thumping and the heavy of our own breathing that we can hear.

'He can't have turned off.' Skeet shines his torch along the walls. 'There haven't been any turn-offs. Not even any doors or ladders. I've been watching real careful.' The tunnel curves and curls, a snail's shell twisting us round and round, and then there's nothing but a wall. Bricked up in front of us, and no Riverman. Not even a handprint.

From up high, daylight pushes through into the drain. 'Maybe this is it. Maybe Miran is up there?' Skeet looks at me.

'Maybe,' I tell him, but it doesn't feel right. Doesn't feel like our Tomorrow is just up there in the light edging in. There was something not right about Riverman, and now I want to stay down here in the dark of the tunnel.

'He must've gone up there then,' Skeet says, shining the torch up the wall. 'There's nothing else for it. There's no other way he could've gone, though how he managed this climb with that leg of his . . . I guess we made him pretty strong and all.'

Holes have been cut into the bricks on the wall, leading into the light and hardly big enough for our feet and fingers to grip on. I pull myself up, ignoring the shake in my arms and the ache in my head and the pulling on my chest, threatening to break me. I think about getting up that wall, and not letting Riverman lose us, and finding Miran.

My head pushes clear from the drain and there's just the river again. No Miran. No Riverman. I stare at the river, at the rain dotting the surface, falling heavy and hard. I remember Skeet's words, *'There's no escaping the drains when it rains,'* and that wild laughing of Riverman's makes sense now. Somehow, he knew.

We pull up and out of the drain, the three of us sitting on the edge, sucking in the air, clean and fresh. The river here isn't as closed in by the wild as it is near our cave. The hill rises up hard behind us, flat, smooth rock that's no good for climbing or running or getting away. And the other side of the river doesn't have a single tree greening it up. Instead, is a line of warehouses, and trucks and parked cars. There are more paths too, and a bridge further up, and roads, all of them calling for eyes to see and ears to hear. Out here, we can be found.

'Well, well, if it isn't bloody drainers.' The voice is thick and dark, coming from down near the river, and Skeet yelps, his nails digging the skin on my arm.

'Scared you, did I? Well then, get down here, let's see you.'

I don't move. Neither does Isa. Skeet puts the binoculars to his eyes and looks down at the ground. 'It's raining.' His voice catches in his throat and comes out all high and broken. 'We can't go back down, Esra, remember the poem?'

The rain thumps down harder at his words. But I'd rather drown in the dark of the drain than be taken again. Rather we both drown than let them take Isa. I stand up, my hand on Isa's shoulder and look down at the voice.

He's old. A white beard, knotted and dirty, and a jacket wrapped tight, protecting him from the rain. He's

153

standing with his hands on his hips, staring at us with hard in his eyes. My hand pulls my sleeve over my wrist. I search my mind for his face, for his eyes or his hands or his voice. I don't think I've seen him before.

There are more of them, two more men and a woman, all sitting on logs and gathered around a metal bin full of fire, burning hot and smoking. A dog is lying on his paws, watching us. I can see his ribs, this dog, and he makes me think again of my fox. Those people look us up and down from their pulled up logs, their fingers wrapping their cups and a heaviness scratched in their eyes. A plastic sheet pulled between trees is keeping the rain from soaking them through, and there's a tent set up behind the fire. These people aren't Snakeskins. This here is a home.

'They're just old bums, Esra. I think we're safer down there than in them drains, don't you?'

My hand itches and I think of my knife. I look again at the ground, at the road and the bridge and back down at the drain. I can hear the water, already rushing furious under us.

'Esra,' Isa says, 'I can't swim,' and there's a fear in his voice I haven't heard before. I nod to Skeet and we jump, my feet slipping on the bank and sliding me to the river.

Rough hands grab at my shirt and pull me back to standing. The old man is pulling me up, his cracked knuckles gripped white to my shirt. I pull from his grip, my legs burning with the ready to run or kick and claw, and my lips pull back to show my teeth. The man smiles at me, like he can see my thinking and finds something funny in there. I turn from his smile and help Isa jump down from the drain.

'We're looking for a man come out of this drain,' Skeet tells them. 'Just a second ago it must've been. We were right behind him we were. Did any of you see where he went? He's a little crazy, like, and has a peg leg, you couldn't've missed him.'

No one says a thing. The old man with the knotted up beard turns to Skeet and shakes his head. 'Neuro diverse,' he says to Skeet.

'What's that then?'

'The word is neuro diverse. You said "crazy", but that isn't the correct term. It's rude it is.'

Skeet looks like a whole bunch of words are stuck in his throat, and all that comes out is a strangled 'Oh.'

The man nods his head. 'Don't know about peg leg. Doesn't sound right though. But no man came out of this drain. Neuro diverse or peg-legged or not. No one ever comes out of that drain. That's why we set up here. So if you're all thinking on telling your little drainer friends about this new tunnel to explore, you can think again. This is our home, got it? So you can all rack off to your little houses and cosy beds and hot dinners and leave us well enough alone. You hear me? Rack off.'

Skeet puffs himself up, and I see that angry storming

his face. I pull on Skeet's arm. 'We need to move anyway. It's too open. Too many people out here.'

'Sorry,' Isa says to the man. He takes my hand and we move away from the fire, following the river again, back to where the trees grow thicker, away from the warehouses and roads and eyes and ears. I can feel Isa shivering, his hand shaking mine with his cold. The sun is just about gone, and that dress of his is wet right the way through.

Skeet follows a step behind, looking back and grumbling to himself about the hospitality of strangers. 'We need to get out of the open. Find somewhere dry,' I tell him.

'Well what are you telling me for?' Skeet glares like I was the one told us to rack off. 'Do I look like I know where the hell we are? I'm bleeding starving and all. If I don't get some food soon I reckon I'll up and die right here. We've been all day with nothing but a croissant each. We missed lunch!'

There's a bark behind us. The dog is stepping at Isa's feet, tail high and ears forward, and Isa sinks into the mud to bury his head in the dog's fur.

'Oi. You kids.' The man has walked up close, his hand reaching for the dog. 'If you all need to get dry, you can use our fire. Don't want your parents coming down here blaming us for you lot catching your death from pneumonia. And your little one is too young to be out and about in this weather. Should be home in bed.'

Skeet looks at me, waiting for an answer I don't have. He sees my fear. He understands. Isa keeps rubbing his head against the dog, his body shivering. My legs start shaking too, like they're only just keeping me standing. But out here is so open. A curl of dizziness shoots through me and pushes at my eyes so hard and fast that I grip Skeet's arm to keep me standing, and suddenly those trees and that dry and that safe feel a long way off.

My head flicks at the man, a single nod, and my body shrinks with that feeling of being cornered, of giving in. 'Are you sure?' Skeet checks, and when I nod again he glares at the old man and stomps his way to the fire, letting them see he's still angry. Isa keeps his hand on the dog, the two of them walking back together, Isa singing to the dog, and the dog licking at Isa's hand.

I don't move. I wait and watch. I won't be trapped. The man looks at me and shrugs. 'We won't bite, girly,' he says. I don't tell him that everyone bites, sooner or later.

Isa and the dog lie down together, a peace settling through them, and the woman hands out plastic boxes of sandwiches and juice. It's the sandwiches that get me walking slowly to the fire, the heat of the fire that melts my legs and sends waves of sleep through every part of me. I chew slowly, forcing myself to stay awake, to keep watch. I won't be trapped.

Skeet takes out that damn toad of his and starts on sharing his sandwich with it, and the three old ones don't even blink with the strangeness of it. Isa doesn't even finish his sandwich before his head has dropped and he's curled himself around that dog, sleeping as calm and peaceful as ever. The woman leans over and rests her hand on his head, her mouth turning to the smallest of smiles. She starts singing then, in words I've never heard, and the look in her eye makes me think that she's in a different place now, her voice taking her back there in a way my remembering never does.

The man with the beard is sitting next to me now, chewing at his sandwich. 'So who you running from then?'

I don't look at the man, don't say a word.

Skeet is laughing with the man next to him, the man's stomach wobbling up and down. 'I've another for you,' the man says. 'So. A cop pulls over this man, and this man's car, it's full of penguins. The cop says to the man, "Take those penguins to the zoo right away before I lock you up." The man says, "OK, yes sir Mister Officer sir," and he drives away. But, the very next day, the cop sees the man again. He's still got the penguins, except now they're all wearing sunglasses. So the cop pulls him over again. "I thought I told you to take those penguins to the zoo?" And the man says, "I did. And today we're going to the beach."'

Skeet just about falls off his log he's laughing so hard.

The man sitting next to me nods. 'Good. Don't tell no one where you're coming from. Safest way. Me, I've been running since I was about your age. Didn't take a little one with me though.' He looks hard at me then, and his hand tight grips my arm, his nails clawing into my skin and he's twisting my arm around to face the fire. He's strong this old man, and even though I'm kicking and pulling he's got me held. I see Skeet jump to his feet. 'Hey!' And my mouth opens to bite down hard on this man's arm, my fingers scratching at his skin, at his face.

But the man has already let me go. He's seen what he was looking for. I fold my arms against my stomach, covering the snake burning bright from my wrist, those letters eating at me, and fear crawling along every bit of my skin. When the man talks, his voice has an iciness that hisses at the warm from the fire and starts me shivering again.

'You can stay here tonight, given the young one's already out. But first light tomorrow you need to move on, you hear?'

'We'll go now,' I tell him, but I don't look at that man again. He takes my chin in his hand and points my face up at the road and the bridge over the river. It's not close, but it's close enough to see the three girls standing against the rail. Not much older than me, those girls.

I know why he's pointing before he even says a word. Those three standing up there, waiting on those cars to stop and give them a job for the night, for a few hours even – those are Orlando's girls shivering in their short skirts and singlet tops, and painted red lips and high heels that ache the backs of their legs from standing all night. It was only luck that kept me from those heels all this time. When Orlando was choosing us for jobs, he picked me out first. Made me stand up tall. He turned me around and lifted my shirt, checking me over for which job I'd suit best. He got down low and looked me in the eye and I told Him loud and clear that I belonged to my family, to my parents and it didn't matter a speck that they were dead. I told Him straight out that He can't make me become this other person, He can't make me do these other things, because I know who I am. He lifted his hand sharp and we all of us waited for it to come down hard for talking that way. I waited for the sting, for my breath to be pushed from my body, for him to knock me down and show us all again what happens. But instead He touched my face, soft and gentle.

I stopped talking then because part of me wanted to go to Him, to be held in his arms and sung to. Part of me wanted Him to make everything OK, because He is all I have now. And part of me wanted Him to hold me and tell me everything is all right because I knew even then how I'd already become this other person He wanted me to become, that somehow I'd changed without even knowing it. Part of me knew I'd do whatever He told me to, no matter the words that flew from my mouth. Because part of me wants to make Him proud. What He said was true. I am just like Him. And the shame of that is big enough to drown me.

I look at those girls, trying to make out from the way they move if I know them, but I can't tell a thing from here.

'We need to go,' I say to Skeet. I try to stand but my legs shake beneath me and I feel the old man pulling me back to the log.

'Easy now. You're safe here for tonight. One of his men was here before,' the old man says quietly. 'Asking them girls if they'd seen you all. Promising the world if they turned you in. They would do too – those girls don't have much promise to hold on to. I don't know what you lot've done, but I'd say you three were in a whole heap of trouble.'

I turn my face away and stare hard at the fire, at the pricks of flame floating to the sky and blinking to black; I stare until my eyes are burning.

'You'd best move into the tent. This fire lights us up pretty good now it's getting dark, and on cold nights like this it's been known for a girl or two to wander on down for a bit of heat in between jobs. You'll be safe in the tent for tonight. But come morning, I want you gone. We don't need no trouble.'

I look into his eyes, that man, and all I can see is fear.

The fire is still burning and the three of us are in the tent. The woman is in here with us too, and the dog, curled again with Isa. But the two men said they'd felt like sleeping outside. They didn't look at us when they

161

said it, but I know they're not sleeping. Those men are watching.

That tired is eating at me, but sleep won't come. I crawl from the tent and the men turn towards me. Neither one says a word. I move away from the fire, behind the tent, the hill at my back, and I look up at the stars and the moon and try not to think. My eyes close and I'm back down in the drain, staring into the picture of home, except now I can see my fox in that home too, waiting for me.

And when my eyes flick open again, he's there, my fox with his torn up ear. Jumped from my dreaming and looking right at me. We are far, far from my cave, and here he is, followed us all the way. He doesn't move, his eyes sucking me in just the same way I'm sucking him in, and just like that I'm back, back all the way to when my teta was saying goodbye, her arms wrapped tight to me and her face full of sad, stabbing and raw.

'Esra,' she told me, 'you must speak for the dead. Speak so their souls may still live in your words and in your heart. Speak so they are never really gone.' She said it like she knew she wouldn't be around to do it herself. And for a long time I did as she said. I spoke their dreams and their wishes and their songs and their cares. I looked after the things they looked after and prayed to the gods they prayed to, and she was right, my teta. I could feel them with me even when I was so alone

162

I thought the world had eaten me up and spat me out in Hell; still I could feel them.

I look at the fox and from far away I can hear my voice whispering out the words echoing in my head. 'I stopped speaking for my dead long ago, fox.' And he looks at me, and knows that I stopped speaking for my dead because I don't want them to see what I have become.

The fox doesn't bark. Doesn't howl out my ache. Just blinks once, and is gone.

Then a voice from the dark behind me whispers, and that man with the beard has moved as quiet as my fox, his whispering eating into me and burning me up from the inside.

'Sometimes,' he says, 'it's not just the dead need speaking for.' He rests his hand on my shoulder, just for a moment, then he walks away, and I'm left alone, staring up at that sky and wishing.

Miran

The pigeon sits silent and still at the window. He watches the people dressed in their too bright whiteness, and too sharp smell, peck and poke at his boy. The boy smiles at them, and they seem pleased. They coo to each other, their voices dripping pride and safety. They think their water dripped into him with their buzzing machines has made him better.

But the pigeon can see the dark green running through the boy's body. There is too much of it. Too much for his body to work out. He can see the colours mixed and confused flowing around the boy, and he knows that those people should not be cooing words of pride and safety. They should be grunting and barking at the danger his boy is in. Why can they not see that there is too much green? That those rounded pieces of rattling hard he was given to eat only made the green stronger and deeper? That the one who gave him the hard was not a too white at all, even though she wore the clothes and looked the same. Her colour was different.

There was ice in her colour. She didn't coo safety, only pride and fear.

The pigeon grunts out a warning, slapping his wings against the window, trying to let them know that his boy needs help, now, before that dark green becomes too strong. But the too whites with their sharp smells don't listen. They flap at the pigeon and shoo him away from the sill, closing the window behind him. And his boy lets the dark green grow stronger.

Skeet

It's pouring with rain. Loads of it bucketing down, it is. I look to Esra and the poor girl has a face could turn a clown to tears. She knows just as good as me that there's no going in those drains this morning. I tell her, just in case she's gone and forgot, but she just fixes me with one of her glares and tells me and Isa to get a move on, that we're off and out and can't stay here any more. It's not even properly light yet, but I know she's right. It's too open here.

I've no idea where we go now. Truth be told, I've no idea where the hell we even are. We could have walked ourselves halfway across the country underground yesterday. It could take us weeks to get back the regular way. Come to think of it, who's to say we weren't weeks under the ground? Who's to say it was only a day or so?

Times like this I wish I hadn't lost the watch my dad left for me before he went away. I'm still not sure that I lost it actually. I'm still of the mind that Mam went and pawned the thing for some more booze just the same way she sold the TV and radio and near about everything in our house that wasn't nailed down. She tried to sell my bed even but couldn't get the damn thing through the door. She reckons my dad never left his watch for me, but I saw him the night he left, and I heard him whispering in my ear to keep it safe for him and he'd be back before I know it. Mam said I was just dreaming and my dad wouldn't ever have left me a damn thing, and just where did I think he'd gone to anyhow? But I know what I heard.

Later she admitted she was wrong. She said I was right, and that he had gone to the wilds of Peru just like I said he had, and that she was sure he'd left his watch, and that it was probably just misplaced was all. She was just jealous he hadn't left her nothing. I know, because when she said all that to me, she had tears in her eyes. She didn't want me to see them, but I did. She can't hide things from me, my mam, no matter how hard she tries. When I find that treasure in them drains, I'm not giving her a cent, no siree. She can go off and find her own bloody treasure.

The old bum with the beard is staring at me like I'm a puzzle he's trying to work out. 'Have you lot got somewhere to wait out this weather?' And he says it like it's my bloody fault.

'We would if I knew where the bloody hell we were. It's the ends of the earth out here, how am I meant to know where to go?'

167

And then the old bugger is laughing like I've told the funniest joke in the world. 'Follow the river along this side until you get to the crossing,' he says to us then. 'Once you're the other side, walk northwards and you'll hit the town centre. You'll not want to go there, but at least that should give you your bearings. If you've a sense of direction in your head, that is.'

'I've a great sense of direction thanks very much,' I tell him back, although truth be told I'm not so sure I do.

The oldies are all gathered outside again, sitting under the tarp to keep dry. The woman gives Esra a black hoody and Esra nods at her. 'I'll give it back,' she says, but the woman's already turned. I don't know the hoody will do much good as a disguise, and the fact of them all worrying at us so much makes me feel even more scared than I did before, and my legs are tingling like they want me to turn tail and run as far from all of this lot as fast as I can. Legs don't know a thing about friendship.

The dog runs to Isa and jumps up on him, his paws on Isa's shoulders and licking his face until Isa starts laughing. The old woman tells Isa the dog don't do that for no one, and so he had better come back soon to visit. Isa buries his head in the dog's fur. I can see him breathing in that dog smell right down into his own self. I take out Croakus and do the same, because that's the thing with toads, they do tend to get just a bit jealous.

Esra pulls at my arm. 'We need to move before it

gets any lighter. Come on, Isa,' and she holds out her hand and Isa takes it just like that, without questioning a thing. He looks back once and waves, and then Esra starts on telling him the joke about the coppers and the penguins and he turns to her and doesn't look back again. I wanted to tell him that joke.

We walk for a bit, following the river like the old codger said, and heading towards those trees, all of us thinking of the rain and how we're doing nothing but getting further away from Miran. Isa looks near to crying, the poor little thing.

'Hey Isa,' I say after a while, 'What did the copper say to his belly button?'

Isa is already smiling and he hasn't even heard the punch line. 'What?' he says.

I put a copper's voice on, to make the joke even better, because jokes are always better with voices. 'You are under a vest,' I say.

Isa stops smiling. Esra stops walking. They're both of them looking at me like they've no idea what I'm on about.

'Get it? You do know what a vest is, right? Like a jumper with no arms? And coppers always say 'You're under *arrest*, but this one tells his belly button it's under "*a vest*"? See? Sounds like "arrest"? Ah forget it, jokes don't work if you have to bloody well explain them.'

It isn't that hard to understand. Jeeez, what is it with these cave kids? It isn't until I've stomped off in

169

front that I hear the two of them laughing. When I turn around, Esra is on the ground sitting in the mud and I wonder if she's totally lost it, but she's just laughing harder than I reckon I've ever seen a person laugh. I didn't know Esra could laugh. Totally bonkers she is. It wasn't that bloody funny.

'You are totally neuro diverse, you two,' I tell them, but I'm laughing now too and I feel mighty good knowing I did this to them. Made them so happy, even if it is just for a minute.

We keep on walking. The river turns a corner and suddenly there's nowhere to walk, just a sharp cliff rising up in front of us, and those trees we've been heading for are taunting us from the top. 'I knew we should never have listened to the stupid old bum. Where's the bloody crossing he was on about? There's no way we can keep going. There's no way up the hill with all the rain. It's a bleeding mudslide.'

Esra looks up the hill then across at the river. There's no road the other side of it now, just a train line running along an empty lot full of weeds and bricks, and I can see from her face that she's working out how safe it would be to hole up in there for a bit.

'There's the crossing,' and she's pointing to an old tree crashed over the river.

'Are you bloody crazy? I mean, neuro diverse? You can't walk on that, you'll fall in! That can't be the crossing, surely not?'

She doesn't even wait to see if I'm agreed to crossing a wet log over a flooded river. Just grabs Isa's hand and leads him straight to it.

'Don't look down,' she tells him. 'There's nothing to it. Just the same as walking on the ground.' Little Isa looks up at her with those great big trusting eyes of his, not even considering that she's leading him to certain death, and just like that, the two of them cross the river.

And now I'm well stuck. I can't stay here by myself now can I, but I'm just about cacking my pants with the fear of it. There's just something about the log and the river water. I'm not scared of water and I'm not even scared of heights, but I'll be blown if I can work out a way to get my legs to move over on to that tree and walk me across same as the other two did.

Croakus grunts from my pocket, and I take him out and hold him up to my ear. 'Croakus reckons it's not a good place to cross,' I tell them. 'He should know, being a toad and all, and every responsible toad owner knows when to listen to your pet. I've written a whole chapter on it for my book.' I nod, all knowledgeable and all, and then bloody Croakus jumps right from my hands on to that log and hops across it, easy as you like. Bloody turncoat. Just wait until I get my hands on his slimy little neck, making fun of me like that after all the flies I've caught for him.

And now they're all looking at me and wondering

why it's taking me so long, and they'll work it out any second, that I'm just a coward. Isa picks up Croakus and gives him a pat. Croakus looks at me and I know he can see me glaring. If he was worried about that toad circus before, he'd best be worried now.

I put a foot on the log and look down to the water rushing under me. I just can't do it. There's just no way. Then Esra is standing there. Right in front of me. She holds my eyes in her eyes and holds my hands in her hands. She smiles at me, and that smile fills me up with a warmth and a braveness I never thought I had. 'Just the same as walking on the ground,' she tells me. 'Look – I'll even do it with my eyes shut.' And she bloody does – one foot feeling in front of her and her eyes closed. Her arms are spread out wide to keep her balance, but she doesn't wobble, not even a bit. Like a bloody tightrope walker she is, then she gets to the end of the log and jumps in the air, flipping over and somersaulting down to the ground. I reckon she got two whole flips in that one jump. When she turns back to me her face is brighter than I've ever seen. There's a real spark in there now. Like she's suddenly woken up and remembered who she is.

'Did you used to be in the circus or what?' I ask her. She smiles again. 'Not yet,' she says, 'but someday I might.'

She walks back to me and takes my hands in hers and looks right at me, her eyes still sparkling. 'Close your eyes.'

'I know you've marbles for brains but hell's bells! Close my eyes? Totally bonkers. There's nothing can make me! I mean—'

She shakes her head, the smallest bit, but she's still holding my eyes, no smiling now. 'Trust me,' she says. 'I won't let you fall. I promise.'

And I guess I must be as bonkers as she is, because I do trust her. My eyes close and my feet walk and Esra's hands are holding mine and when I open my eyes again I've done it. I've crossed the river with my eyes closed and I did it just because Esra Merkes said I could.

We don't none of us say a thing, then Esra does another flip in the air. The show-off.

'Can you juggle and all?' I ask. Esra thinks for a bit. 'I used to be able to,' she says. 'But only four things at a time.' And I don't know if she's joking or not. I don't care either. A bubble of happiness so big I feel like I'm flying pushes through my body, and my sixth sense tells me that I can flip just as good as Esra with that feeling pumping through my veins.

And when I end up on my arse in the mud, and Isa and Esra laughing harder than they were even before, that happy feeling just goes on getting bigger and bigger, and I don't even care that it looks to me like Croakus is laughing and all.

Esra

We're not safe. It's just about light and even with the hoody hiding me inside, all it needs is one pair of eyes to see me. To see Isa. We need to hide. Somewhere we can wait out the rain. The empty lot might be the best place for it. There are no dogs I can see, and the grass is long enough to hide us. I take Isa's hand and check the fence for loose wire to scrape under.

'Oi,' and suddenly there's an arm pushing me hard against the wire of the fence, pressing against my throat, and a face red and angry, teeth bared and eyes flashing.

'What are you—' Skeet is yelling and pulling at the arm, and my legs are kicking strong and fierce, but I think I get Skeet instead because he yells and falls to the ground. Then the arm loosens and I see the boy it belongs to. His hair shaved tight against his head and a white scar running long down his face. Now the boy is on the ground, trying to crawl backwards and away from Isa who has his teeth locked on his leg and is growling like Orlando's dogs.

'Get off me you little—' and I can see his foot raising high to stomp Isa into the ground and I'm on this boy, and now it's me pinning him to the ground with my teeth flashing and I can feel my tail bushing and my ear torn and I bark sharp and sure.

'What did you attack us for?' Skeet hisses, and he's found a stick and is pointing it in the boy's face.

The boy raises his chin, his eyes staring calm right at me. He's no older than me, this boy, just bigger is all. 'What are you doing with Em's hood?' He looks at me when he asks, and there's no fear in his eye, just a sort of sureness.

'She gave it,' and I give him another push before standing up. 'Isa,' I tell him, 'he's just a street rat. Come on,' and I see Isa's jaws bite hard once more before he lets go, wiping the boy's blood from his mouth.

'Why would she do that then?'

'What's it to you?' Skeet says, still waving the stick around in the boy's face. The boy grabs the stick and rips it from Skeet's hands, throwing it over the fence and into the weeded up lot. Skeet takes a step back. He's no idea what these street rats are like.

Isa has moved up close to the boy and is looking him all over.

'How do you know them then?' Skeet asks, all the brave gone from his voice.

The street rat keeps his eyes on me, then turns slowly to Skeet. 'They're my people,' he says. I didn't know street rats had people. We were always told they had no one. We were always told they were no one.

'I know you,' Isa says softly, and his fingers have lifted up to touch the boy's face. 'At the foster home. You sang a song to get me to sleep.' Isa sings a bit, the same song he sang to the plants and the fire and the dog. The boy shrugs and slaps Isa's hand away.

'Maybe. I sang lots of kids songs.'

'Silviu. That's your name, right? I remember your socks.' Isa points to the boy's socks, bright red with a picture of Snoopy smiling and waving. They look strange on this boy. Street rats don't usually wear socks. The boy looks harder at Isa.

'You're the runners aren't you? The Snakeskins?'

Skeet puffs himself up. 'And so what if we are? What's it to you?'

The boy looks at Skeet. 'Except you. You're no Snakeskin,' and all the puff whistles out of Skeet and he looks down at his feet.

'Is that why Em gave you her hood? To hide you? It won't fool them, you know.'

I turn from the street rat. 'Come on Isa.' But Isa is still staring at the boy and I can see from his face that he's still hearing that song playing in his ears.

'Silviu. Do you know where Miran is? We need to find him so we can go home to the sea and the bread and all the cakes we can eat and all the tea we can drink.'

'Miran? Is he the ones the cops took?'

Skeet is tugging on my arm now and hissing in my ear. 'If he's no Snakeskin, how come he knows so much? How does he know about Miran being taken by the cops then?'

'He's a street rat.' I shrug Skeet's hand off my arm. And now the boy is crouched down and smiling at Isa.

'I do remember you. You're the one went with that man down the park.'

Isa nods. 'He said he was a friend of my abbi's and talked to me in the old language. He knew my name and said he was my uncle and that he'd been looking for me. He said . . .' Isa stops talking and touches the boy's face again. 'He said my teta hadn't died like I thought. That she was waiting for me. That she was sick and needed me. He said we had to go now. He said I couldn't tell the foster house 'cause they weren't allowed to let me see my teta unless she had her papers, but all our papers were burnt. He said.'

The boy takes hold of Isa's hand in his own. He looks at him, then nods.

'I'll ask around. Someone'll know where they took your Miran. I'll find out where he is for you.' The boy stands up and looks me up and down, then turns to Skeet. 'But I want your binoculars for it.'

'Deal,' Skeet says, without even a pause, and holds out his hand for the boy to shake. The boy just laughs. 'Well? Hand them over then.'

'Not a chance!' Skeet looks at that boy like he's

nothing but dirt. 'You'll just nick off with them then. I'll give them to you when you find something out for us.'

The boy shrugs, like it means nothing to him, what Skeet says. 'I'll meet you tonight at Em's then. Don't forget the binoculars.' He messes Isa's hair and chews on his lip, thinking a bit. Then he turns back to me.

'This lot's no good for hiding. There's a guard comes past every hour or so. He's got a dog. But here, if you ever need it. She's one of the good ones.' The boy puts a card in my hand. It's got a phone number on it and a name. *Detective Sergeant MacIntyre.*

I shake my head and push the card away. 'Nah. Coppers don't help us.'

The boy shrugs his shoulders. 'Like I said, she's one of the good ones. Her and Blake. They set up the food vans and stop the others from pushing us out of the train stations at night. They've set up a youth centre and everything. And they listen. But whatever.'

The boy takes the card back and I turn away. When I look back, Isa is holding the card tight in his hand, his eyes struggling to make out the words.

'You could come home with us,' Isa says then. 'Couldn't he, Esra?'

The boy looks at me. I don't answer. The boy starts walking. 'I might,' he calls back to Isa. 'It sounds nice, your home.' And when he walks away we can hear him singing Isa's song.

Skeet looks down to the river and to the train tracks,

and the road edging us in further on, then he's jumping and pointing down the street. 'I don't believe it. I know where we are!' He smiles. 'It's not far to my house from here. We can hide out at mine. There's no chance of your Snakeskins finding you there. Then as soon as the weather's all cleared up, we'll head straight back under and head back to the picture of the mountain and the bird. Riverman will be waiting for us there, for sure. And if it hasn't stopped raining, we'll go back tonight to the hobo camp and that Silviu kid. He might come up with something, you never know.'

'How far?' There's an itching at me, pushing at me, telling me that any second now they'll find us, and I can taste the blood from where I've chewed the inside of my cheek raw, and there's a voice in my head telling me that Miran is waiting, and here we are flipping over logs and laughing at jokes while he sits, rotting and waiting and believing that I'll find him. That voice hisses how wrong he is to believe in me. That voice hisses at who I really am.

Isa looks at me. 'We can't go back down with all this rain, Esra. I can't swim.'

'We're not far.' Skeet looks along the road. 'Maybe five minutes is all. It's safer than anywhere. No one knows to look for you at mine.'

We walk along the track leading us on to the road, our steps getting faster. Skeet finds an old roller skate washed up in the gutter and he puts it on his foot and gets Isa to pull him down the street, bent forward with one leg held high in the air. 'See? I told you I'd be good in the circus. Show me some more stuff, Esra. I bet you know loads more you just aren't sharing.'

I shake my head. There is no smiling left.

'Will you teach me then? Later? We could join the circus together, make our own even. What do you reckon?'

A car passes and slows and Isa turns to rock next to me. For a second, my brain fools me into seeing Orlando behind the window. When the car moves on, there are tears on Isa's face and his legs are shaking.

'It's not far, Isa,' Skeet says and rubs his shoulder.

I look at Isa shaking and crying, and think of Miran's Tomorrow Stories, of him Whispering Isa out of The Jungle. But I'm no Whisperer. Skeet is telling him another joke, but Isa won't listen, those tears still falling and his shivering shaking at that little body of his so he can't even walk. He is so little. Too little for all this.

'Isa,' I say, then I tip over on to my hands, legs pointing straight at the sky, and I walk down the street. I don't last as long as I used to, but it's enough to get Isa to stop crying, and slow his shaking just a bit, and when Skeet tries and falls over again, Isa smiles and holds my hand.

'I'll be the lion tamer,' Isa says. 'And you can be the clown, Skeet.' He laughs just a little. It's so easy to make little ones forget.

Skeet keeps his arm on my shoulder all the way, and when I shove it off he doesn't even notice, just wraps it right around again, talking at us the whole time and trying to remember more jokes for Isa, which are worse and worse with each one he tells.

We turn down a street and Skeet stops talking. He looks at the ground and his steps get slow and heavy.

'Well, here we are.' Skeet looks to the house in front of us. He kicks the roller skate off his foot and leaves it lying in a puddle by the door. There's a light coming from inside, and music so loud I can hardly hear Skeet's muttering.

'At least she won't bother asking us anything.' Skeet shakes his head. 'Well come on then, haven't you ever seen a house before?' His arm isn't on my shoulder any more. Now he's all hunched and stiff. He kicks open a door around the side and Isa moves in close to me and starts sucking at the skin on the back of his hand. 'I want my jumper,' he whispers. I nod and we follow Skeet inside.

That door looks like it's been kicked just about every time someone walks through, and there's a hole down the bottom just about the size of Skeet's foot. We walk into a kitchen, dirty plates piled on the benches and a sink full of rot and a red envelope with FINAL NOTICE sticking out from a too full bin. Skeet opens the fridge, but there's nothing inside except an apple with a bite already taken from the middle and a pile of dead cockroaches. Skeet doesn't close the fridge behind him.

The room with the light on and the music shouting has the door shut tight. I can hear someone singing on the other side. Skeet doesn't even turn his head, just walks past and up the stairs and into a bedroom, small and dark, the floor covered in clothes and towels and more plates. We follow and when Isa steps through, Skeet slams the door shut and the whole wall shakes.

'You know, I've been thinking. After we find your Miran, maybe I should take off and head to those wilds of Peru with my dad after all. Can't be worse than living here. You could come too, you know. All of you. You'd love my dad. He's real great he is. He can teach us everything he knows.' He looks at me for an answer.

I shrug, but Isa says, 'We can't. We're going home.'

'Well, maybe I'll come with you and all then,' he says. I shrug again.

'Right then, clothes.' Skeet stars shoving clothes around the floor. He pulls out a pair of jeans and a t-shirt with a shark on it. 'You can wear these while we dry out the hoody, but you're not getting my underwear. I've got to draw the line somewhere. And Isa, maybe you should put your jumper back on until your dress dries out.'

Then he walks out of the room and leaves us to get changed. It feels strange, being in a house, wearing Skeet's clothes. I finger over the picture of the shark and wonder. This house, it doesn't feel the way a home is supposed to feel. It feels like the houses we cleaned. Cold and dead, like all the living was sucked out of its bricks long ago.

But the window looking out makes me think of my room back home. It was my brother's room too. We'd sit at the window and play two-card poker instead of going to sleep. He taught me how to wish on stars at that window, pointing up to the sky and whispering our dreams. He wanted to play football. He could have, too. He could beat anyone. *'You'll come to every one of my games won't you, Esra?'*

When Skeet comes back, all in dry clothes and with that green scarf of his still wrapped around his neck, I stand up and nod. 'Of course you can. Come home with us. You can even bring your stupid toad.'

And Skeet smiles at me and says to his pocket, 'Did you hear that, Croakus? We're off to the beach, we are.'

He's carrying a box of cornflakes and a jar of peanut butter. 'No milk, but they're not bad dry.' He sits on the bed and dips his finger into the peanut butter. 'I've a secret stash,' he says. 'I should have some crackers around here too, somewhere.'

'It's fine,' I tell him.

Isa doesn't say a word, but he dips his finger in the peanut butter and smiles, his teeth all covered in brown.

'We'll have to figure out some disguises too. I reckon I could get my hands on some hair dye maybe, or we could try to turn you into looking like a boy somehow. I could give you a moustache with my marker. They'd never know you then.'

The music turns off. There are footsteps downstairs, thumping and slow, then the sound of something heavy being dropped.

'Skeet? Skeeeeeeeeeet?'

Skeet doesn't answer. He walks to the bedroom door and shoves a chair under the handle to stop it opening. He doesn't say a word. There is another thump and the music starts up again.

'Who's that in the picture?' Isa asks. 'Is that your cousin who went in the drains?'

Skeet looks up and his face turns soft. Isa doesn't know not to ask, that some things aren't worth remembering. 'Nah, it's my brother. He went and got himself drowned, the stupid bugger.'

I shake my head at Isa, but he ignores me. 'Was it in the drain?'

'Nah, we were down the river, the two of us. We weren't supposed to be 'cause Mam and Dad were out to lunch or something, and Pauly and me were supposed to stay inside. But that day was so hot and that river so cool, what did they expect us to do? I was only a little bug of a thing and couldn't swim right yet. I guess I went in too deep because one second I was there and the next thing I know I'm under that water with my little arms and legs going crazy, trying to catch hold of something.' He looks at the photo again.

'They tell me Pauly came in to save me. I woke up on the bank and Pauly wasn't anywhere. I was right mad too, thinking he'd buggered off and left me alone. Anyways, they found his body washed up three days later, all the way down the river. He was all tangled up in branches. A fisherman found him. Do you know something though? Under that water was so dark, and there was just this little bit of light right up the top but too far away for me to get near. I remember, that even though I was scared and all, I remember thinking it looked kind of magic or something. Like a dream, you know?'

I look back out the window, at the rain still pouring from the sky. And suddenly all that tired is gulping at me, swallowing me whole. I feel myself lie back on the bed. It's so, so soft, wrapping around me. I wonder if I ever had a bed like this one. I think I did. Maybe. Skeet says something about at least asking, and I try to answer, but my mouth won't work. And the bed is warm, and I'm dry, and there's cornflakes and peanut butter in my stomach and . . .

My eyes shut, and my body heavies me down to sleep.

There are voices, loud, pumping up the stairs and through the door. There's the sound of glass smashing and a man laughs, and in my head I'm back in The Jungle and it's Orlando's thumping and yelling that I hear. My body freezes and starts shaking, my fingers reaching for Miran.

Skeet grabs my hand and looks at me. 'You OK?'

The black behind my eyes fades to grey, and my breathing starts up again.

'We're safe,' Isa whispers in my ear. I smile at him then think of Miran, not here, not safe. Outside the rain thunders, heavy and loud.

Skeet is by the door now, his ear pressed to the wood. His face is twisting like he's too many thoughts in his head. 'I don't bloody believe it! It's . . . it's him!' He's smiling, his eyes wide and bright, and now he's shouting, 'It's my dad! He's back! He's come back for me!' Isa and I mirror that smile right back at him, and my heart aches just a little from Skeet finding the home he's been looking for.

His fingers scramble at the chair and he throws it upside down on the pile of clothes, and he pulls that door just about off its hinges opening it the way he does. Skeet's feet pound down the stairs. I pull my shirt and hoody over the shark top, my fingers gripping tight to the knot, and reach for my shoes, still wet, but shoes. Isa has already pulled his shoes back on. He knows as well as me, we need to be leaving this place. There are too many eyes here now. We follow Skeet down the stairs, keeping to the shadows against the wall. I pull Isa to me, my legs readying to run.

'Dad! You're back!' Skeet crashes into the man,

his arms wrapped around his waist, his head shoved hard into his belly, and for the smallest of moments, I remember what that feels like. For the smallest of moments, I remember my abbi holding me tight and smiling down at me. For the smallest of moments, I remember what it is to be safe and loved and never alone.

Skeet is holding his dad as hard as he can. His dad throws his arms in the air, stopping the drink in his bottle from splashing the floor.

'Damn, boy. You've grown,' he says. He doesn't put his arms down to wrap Skeet in. He doesn't hold him tight and smile right back at him. He doesn't do a thing to make Skeet feel safe and loved and never alone. He just sniffs and takes another long drink.

'Hell's bells, Dad! You're back! It couldn't be better timing neither. I was just now saying I think it's time I come and live with you, 'cause to be honest, it hasn't been all cherry trees and roses since you left, no offence, Mam.' Skeet is talking so fast he isn't even noticing the look his dad is giving him, or the way his mam is rubbing at her head like there's a pain in there she can't drive out.

'Did you find the plant then? In the wilds of Peru? Have you brought it back, or are you just here on holiday? It doesn't matter anyway, 'cause I'll still come with you, wilds or no wilds. And you'll never guess what—'

Skeet's dad pushes him away, shaking his head.

'What the damn fool are you on about, boy?' He turns to Skeet's mam then, an anger lighting up his face. I've seen anger like that light up before. I move just inside the room and pull on Skeet's arm, but his eyes are on his dad like he can't work out this world he's found himself in. My gut turns in on itself, feeling for him the way he feels now, my heart aching out a million times more than before and I wish stronger than ever that he'd found his home, that he hadn't been fooled.

'What damn lies have you been filling that boy's head with, woman?' Skeet's dad shakes his bottle at Skeet's mam, and she shakes her head right back, her voice all screech tight and angry. There's a scared in there too.

'Should I have told him the truth then? That you'd rather your new woman with her swollen belly than spending any more time with us? That you couldn't even find a single day these last three years to spend with your son, even though you lived not more than ten minutes down the damn road? That you don't even pay a cent to helping raise the fool boy? Just dump him on me like I've got no problems of my own to be dealing with. Do you have any idea what it's like trying to get through to that boy?'

Skeet takes a step back, pushing up against me. He's shaking his head slow and scared, tears falling from his face, and he is just now understanding all his mam's on about.

'Anyways, I didn't tell him a single damn thing. He

went and invented the father he wanted all on his own in that wonky brain of his.'

They keep up their shouting, the two of them spitting words at each other. Skeet turns and looks at me, his fingers nailing into my arm. 'He's wearing his watch,' he whispers. 'His watch. He didn't leave it for me. Because he's wearing it.'

I nod and my eyes tear up with the pain Skeet's holding. Without another word, Skeet turns. He grabs Isa and pulls us back through the kitchen and out the door. Just before we leave, I turn back to the house. His dad is there in the kicked open doorway, smoking on his cigarette and watching us go.

'What are you doing hanging around with him anyway?' he says to me then, his voice grit hard. 'He's an idiot, just like his mother. What do you think, Skeet? That this girl's your friend? Why would she be friends with someone like you? You're crazy. Something wrong with your brain.'

Skeet has stopped walking and he's just standing, staring at his shoes. He won't look at me. His dad nods, smiling through his cigarette, that smoke creeping up my nose and filling my bones with remembering. 'I'd get rid of him now, girly, before he drags you down with him.'

'You don't deserve Skeet.' I say it quiet, but with a strong that sends my words hard into that man's ears. 'He's got more brave in his toenail than you ever will in your whole body. You're not worth the dirt on his shoe. And the word isn't "crazy". It's neuro diverse.' Then I look that man right in the eye and spit all my hate right at him. And when that spit hits his shoe, he's stuck there looking at it, like he doesn't quite understand what it means. Then I wrap my arm tight around Skeet's shoulders.

His dad doesn't even see us leave.

Miran

Miran is flying. The flock sweeps around him, in and out like the breathing of the earth. He feels his body tunnelling through the sky, feels the wind pushing, ruffling, carrying, the fingers of wind weaving over him, guiding him in a softened purple glow of peace.

Miran's eyes open. The world is blurred. Miran blinks, long and slow, trying to clear the fog wrapped around his head. The bird is there, framed in the window, then flying circles around his head, its blue eyes holding Miran. The bird grunts and Miran can tell from the growl in its cry that it is a warning call, that there is danger.

Miran concentrates on manoeuvring himself to his space on the floor. His body feels so, so heavy and disjointed, like his entire being is working out of time. He tears another piece from his hospital gown and ties a knot. 'Find Esra,' he whispers, and drops it down the grate.

There is a flutter of wings and the bird is once

again nesting against Miran, its head rubbing his fingers. Miran begins, his voice barely a whisper. 'In a time long forgotten, in a place nobody knows . . .' And when Miran can go on no longer, he breathes in the air through the grate, feeling his lungs struggling, his stomach aching and twisting, the heat rising in his body. That heaviness beneath the drain grows darker, and suddenly Miran realises what it is down there. It is Death, waiting for him, waiting to ferry his body across the rising river to the other side. Miran is so exhausted that this thought doesn't frighten him at all. Instead, it fills him with a great sense of relief.

As if knowing Miran's thoughts, fingers rise up from the drain. Miran reaches out and touches the fingers. They are warm, and soft. Miran was expecting something cold. Something dead. Death pushes his hand all the way through the grate, his wrist long and scarred. 'You have been waiting,' Miran whispers. 'They think I'm getting better, but I'm not. I can feel it. My body is closing, isn't it? Stopping.' Miran takes the hand in his own, and gentlies the palm with his fingers. Death, in turn, grips Miran's hands in his fist, and squeezes, softly, lovingly, and the weariness Miran had been keeping at bay weighs him down so that his head slaps against the cold metal of the grate.

His stomach is aching again, worse even than before, and the beating of his heart is pounding loudly in his ears. He can hear the rain thundering down outside and hitting the window, and he realises that it is the full black of night now, and that the window is closed, that his bird isn't here with him at all, and that there is no one holding his hand, no one to ferry him to the other side.

And suddenly, Miran feels terribly, horribly alone.

Esra

We don't say a word. Not one. Skeet keeps walking faster and faster back along the streets, back towards the river and Em's camp. The sky is close to darkening and the rain is softer now than before. The air is full of storm, unsettled and wild, with the smell of animal sharp on the wind. I wonder if it is safe yet, to go back underground. I wonder what Silviu has found.

Skeet's turned deaf to the whole world and he's running ahead of us now. I pick Isa up and swing him on to my back, not letting Skeet out of my sight, watching him stomp out every hope he ever had with each step he takes. He stops before the river crossing, watching that water rage underneath. And when he steps out on to that log there's not a speck of being scared about him. He stops halfway across, staring into the black rushing beneath our feet.

'Skeet—'

He doesn't turn. Croakus growls from inside his pocket. Skeet blinks and reaches down to pat the toad.

'You're right, Croakus. Nothing but a piece of—' Then he shakes his head and he unwraps that long green scarf from around his neck.

'He gave this to me, when I was little,' he says. 'I thought it meant something.' Skeet stretches his arm out and watches the scarf catching in the wind. Then his fingers let go, and we watch that scarf float for a second on the air, then disappear into the dark of the water.

Skeet steps slowly to the bank, his body falls to the ground, and he curls up into a ball in the mud, his breathing heaving in and out and the smallest of whimpers leaking into the sky. I put my hand on his back. 'It's like the toad said,' I tell him. 'He's not worth a thing.'

Then Isa pushes his mouth right close to Skeet's ear. 'What do you get when you cross a snowman with a vampire?' Isa says, his hand moving circles on Skeet's back. Skeet doesn't answer.

'Frostbite,' Isa whispers. Skeet lifts his face, all red and smushed.

'That's without doubt the worst ever joke I've ever heard,' he says. 'I mean, hell's bells. *Frostbite?*' He chokes back a laugh, and snot comes out his nose. Isa stands up and puts his hand in mine. I wonder where he heard that joke.

We don't say another word, not the whole way back to the camp. It isn't raining now, and those dark clouds are stretching themselves thinner. I reckon we can go back under. We can find Miran, and if Silviu isn't there already, we won't wait.

We smell the smoke from the fire before we reach the camp, calling to us with its warm, and we stop a second, waiting for the dog to greet us, for someone to wave us all forward. But there's nothing, and all around the fire is dead and silent. The tent is crushed to the ground, the logs and sleeping bags pushed down to the river and all the cups are smashed and stomped in the dirt. I pull Isa away, folding his body into mine so he doesn't see the dog lying dead and broken in the bushes.

'Esra . . .' Skeet is on the ground, scrambling to pull back the tent, his voice high and cracked. I see the legs first. The red socks and Snoopy smiling and waving.

'He's – he isn't breathing. There's not a pulse. Esra. He's—' Skeet's hands are red with blood, his eyes pulled wide and he's pushing on Silviu's chest, trying to get him back to some kind of living. Isa looks at the body. At the shaved head and white scar. At the snake painted in blood across Silviu's cheek. He doesn't say a word, and his face turns blank and empty.

'Leave it.' I pull Skeet back. 'He's dead. Leave him be.' Skeet tries to brush the flies from Silviu's body, from his face, from the blood, from the hole in his head. He pushes at Silviu's hair, trying to cover over the hole, but the blood is too thick, sticking the hair in clumps. I hear the echo of the bullet and Silviu's eyes stare into my soul and join all the others.

Skeet takes the binoculars slowly from his neck, and rests them on Silviu's chest, curling the dead fingers around them. 'He, uh,' Skeet starts, his words choking him. 'On his hand. He wrote something. It – it says, *Overflow Room 1, P. Guard.*'

Isa doesn't look at me, his voice soft. 'He brought a bag. He was coming home with us.' And all I can do is nod and wonder at the way Silviu's mouth is turned up, just a bit, like he's smiling at being dead.

'We have to— We need— Shouldn't we— We should call someone?' Skeet says.

I feel my head shake, hear my words like someone else is talking them. 'To them he's just another street rat. What do they care?' And a hard burns in my gut and the roaring is starting up again, getting louder and stronger, and I hear the old man telling me that sometimes it's the living that need talking for. I don't reckon a single person ever talked for Silviu. Not one.

I close my eyes, try to quiet the roar, and something in me twitches. I feel my ribs poke from my skin, the wind edging my fur and sending the smells of trees and grass and cold, wet dirt swirling over and around me. There is the taste of the wild on my tongue and the music of freedom in my ears. My feet tell of a hundred journeys gone and a thousand more to come, and when I tip back my head and howl, the ache of it cracks the moon wide open, and the stars fall from the sky, every one.

I know now, what has to happen. I know now, what

I have to do. And my fox's strong pushes through every part of me. I will not forget.

I wipe the snake from Silviu's face, his blood staining my shirt red. And when I start to drag at his body, pulling him down the bank, Skeet and Isa help and together we take Silviu to the river. The water pulls at his body, then he's floating and spinning, fast and furious in the water, disappearing.

'Now you can go home,' Isa whispers, and he sings his song, Silviu's song, into the water.

I take a rock from the river and walk back to the camp. The rock is sharp, cutting into my skin until my blood is mixing with Silviu's and I scratch into the bin, the metal hot against my hand.

He smiles in death,
Knowing that his body
In the water
Will fall as rain on those of us left living.
He smiles,
Knowing he lived free.

I look up at the road and the bridge. I can just make out two girls waiting. One of them is looking down at us, watching. I don't turn away.

Isa follows my eyes. He raises his hand high towards the girls, then takes the rock from my hand and sits in the dirt, scratching his own words, his own goodbye.

His nam is Silviu. He is 12 yeers old. He sang me a song.

Skeet is next to us now, and Isa hands him the rock. Skeet looks at the rock in his hand, and he nods.

He helped us just because he could, Skeet writes. Then he throws the rock into the river.

Isa stands and wipes the dirt from his hands. 'It's stopped raining,' he says. We help each other up on to the lip of the drain, not one of us looking back at the camp or over at the bridge, and together we climb down the wall, down into the dark.

Skeet

This isn't right. This world. Everything's turned loopy and all out of whack. My hands won't stop shaking neither and even Croakus is trembling in my pocket. When I saw Silviu, lying like that, everything turned real quiet and still, like I was stuck in a nightmare or something. I felt kind of calm and grown up. But now all that noise is crashing over me, and my head is buzzing, actually buzzing like a whole swarm of bees has taken over my brain. If he'd been wearing those binoculars, would he have seen them coming? If I'd just handed them over like he asked then maybe he wouldn't be lying dead now. He didn't do nothing, that kid. He was only asking. He had his bag. He was coming with us. And there's no reason for it. No damn reason in the world. I get it now, why Mam drinks all the damn time. She's trying to make sense of the world, isn't she? Trying to make it right again.

Not that I care about Mam anymore. Or any of them. Not after Silviu. Those two good-for-nothing lying drunks with not even a half a brain between them can go jump in the lake for all I care. I'm done with families. Finished. This is my family now and a better one than those two've ever been.

Croakus and me are going home with Esra and Isa and Miran. I don't even know where that home is, but I don't care. It's away from here and that's all that matters. I'll get to see the beach. And we'll start that circus. I keep telling myself about the circus and the beach but Silviu's head is just there, floating in front of me, sucking the air right out of my lungs. It's like I said before. You can't unsee a damn thing.

The water is a lot higher in these drains than it was before and it's pushing at our legs and pulling us along, and I tell my brain to think on the aching of my legs and the pushing of the water so I don't have to think on Silviu. We take turns having Isa on our backs, but we're soaked right through to our bellies from the water. We should've brought more supplies. 'I never drew on the moustache for you,' I tell Esra. She grunts and stops walking.

'How far was it? When we were following Riverman?'

I shrug, and Esra takes Isa from her back and flashes her torch up and down the drain. 'We've been going too far. We should have hit the picture by now. I'm sure of it.'

'Maybe it just feels longer, what with the water so high and all.' But even as I'm saying it, I'm thinking that

Esra is right. We've been walking an awful long way through these here drains.

'Let's keep going for a bit. You can't tell time down here is all. It must be further on,' I tell her. Her eyebrow rises, but she doesn't argue. Just pulls Isa on to her back again and pushes on, following that drain twisting and turning, until we've gone so far that there's no doubting it any more. This is miles further than before.

'We must have missed the turn-off,' I say, and even I can hear my voice catching in my throat. It would be pitch black night out there now, and there's something extra scary about knowing this dark won't end when we come out. Shouldn't make a difference. But it does.

'There weren't any turn-offs. You said so yourself. It was only the one tunnel. There's something not right. This isn't right. It's not the—' Esra doesn't say the word. Like just saying it makes it true. She looks at me instead, and I know just what she's thinking. *It's not the same tunnel.* It doesn't make a speck of sense, but this tunnel we're in now, it's not the same tunnel as the one we came out of yesterday.

I move closer to those two and Esra doesn't move away. 'What do we do now?' And even her voice is shaking.

'Well. We either go on, or we go back.'

There's nothing for it. Not one of us is going back, no matter how long the drain goes on. We could turn to mole kids before we'd turn back.

The drain gets taller again and now there's not even any pretending. This drain is nothing like before. There's been no picture, no turn-offs, and now just like that the drain splits in two, and these great big arches reach high over the tunnels. One of them has *HELL* written on it in great big river stones. Someone's idea of a joke I'm guessing. The other arch has *STYX* written above it, and even though we haven't had a group meeting to decide on which way to go, Esra and Isa have already headed up that way. Esra stops under the arch and turns to me. 'Look,' she says and flashes her light on to the wall. 'There's his handprint. Riverman's. He's down here. I know it.' And even though she's not actually asking me a thing, she's waiting for me to agree, which is as close to asking as I figure I'll ever get. I don't tell her I would have followed her whichever way she chose, even all the way to *HELL*.

'I saw it already,' I tell her. 'I was just about to say did you want to try this way 'cause of the handprint.' I don't tell her that I was beginning to wonder if maybe that Riverman isn't with us any more. That maybe he turned back to river water when we were chasing him yesterday. How else did he disappear like that? I don't tell her though. The longer she can hope on him the better.

Esra nods at me and Isa holds out his arms so he can have a go on my back, and even though that buzzing in my head hasn't stopped and I feel a hurt so hard from all of everything, there aren't two people in the whole world I'd rather be with right now.

The tunnel leads around and around, and this tunnel isn't like a proper drain anymore. The walls aren't made of cement or bricks, but great big bright-blue boulders that shine up all the water by our feet. The boulders have been all patterned too, swirling in waves along the wall, so it feels we've somehow found our way deep down into the very heart of the river.

The tunnel opens up into a set of stairs, and all of that blue still patterning up the walls. We stop a moment to breathe it in, then we start real slow up those steps. There's a heaviness in my chest now, like it's harder to breathe with each step we take. Esra holds my hand. And when the stairs open up into a kind of cavey chamber-room thing, we all just stop and stare, and that heavy feeling in my chest gets even heavier.

I've never in my whole life seen anything like this room before. The floor is made from them blue boulders, curling all around us, and all up the walls and on the floor and hanging from the roof are candles, there must be hundreds of them, all of them burning bright, their shadows flicking on to the bricks, and making me feel like we're not alone, like those shadows belong to something. And in between all them candles, all along one wall is a rock shelf cut into the blue, and on that shelf is a whole collection of things, sitting there like an exhibit in a museum or something.

I look at Esra, but she's moved into the room, staring at a patch of colour lit by the candles. The walls are covered in pictures, all mosaicked together from bits and pieces, and the way the shadows run across them make them seem real somehow. Like they're more than just junk stuck on a wall. There's only one person could make pictures come to life like that. This here must be Riverman's lair.

The picture Esra's staring at is of a circus, all the colours of the tent pushing out of that picture and the smile on her face is growing the longer she stares.

I look around the room at all the candles and pictures and objects, wondering at how he did it. Wondering if maybe he's been alive before somehow, to gather all of this here like he has. Like maybe we're not the first ones to have brought him to life. There's a picture right near the shelf. It's just a small one, but there's something about it that calls me over, twisting my belly and making me think that there is something there I'm missing. It's nothing special. Just a picture of hands holding a wooden box. Two big hands and two small, and sitting on the box is another one of those dirty pigeons. There's something about that picture though, and I put my own hand over the top of one of the smaller hands and feel the glass pricking my palm. My hand fits perfectly on top, and for a second, it's like my hand has become part of the picture.

Isa is looking at a picture too, all curled on the floor,

staring up at a huge scene stretching all the way to the ceiling. There's a woman sitting down in the middle of a crowd of people, and all around her is a bunch of birds, all different colours and sizes and all. I shine my torch up the wall, and when my light hits on a bird at the very top of the picture, I feel a cold creep up my back. There's something not quite right about this bird. And watching, just like that, the bird's head turns and it looks me up and down with its little black eyes, and when I yell from the fright of it, there's a mad flapping and squawking and a whole lot of them birds have turned to real right in front of our very eyes and are slapping and swooping, and I'm more scared than ever and all of sudden, just like that, I want my mam.

'It's OK,' Esra says, and she holds my shoulder. 'They're just birds and bats that've nested down here, that's all.'

But it isn't all. Because I can smell him now, I can hear his breathing, and just like that, he's standing there, right behind Esra, his arms raised high in the air, his face raised to the birds and the bats.

Riverman looks at me, and he smiles.

Esra

Riverman stares straight at us. He smiles and opens his arms wide, welcoming us to his underground kingdom with the birds and the bats and the rats and the cockroaches scuttling our feet, and the air thick and heavy with his smell. There is a beauty down here that I didn't know existed.

Riverman doesn't make any noise, just leads us to the stone shelf. He's picking up the bits and pieces from the shelf and showing them to us. Small treasures, but all of them shouting out a living. A rock, smooth and round at one end and sharpened to a knife's edge at the other, and I can feel how this would have sliced skin and muscle from bone, I can feel its story, the energy from every hand that held it and touched it and passed it on. There's a bowl and a necklace and a small statue and all of them older than I can imagine, and that collection makes me feel like we're standing in a cave right back at the beginning of time. Holding those things, it's like I'm remembering something about those people, like they've been brought back to living, and for just a moment, they still exist.

'I told you there was treasure down these drains, didn't I?' Skeet says in my ear.

And looking at all those things, that museum of memories living on the walls of the drain, it's like something inside me lights up. A need to weave my own Tomorrow Story. I'm remembering, from years gone back, my abbi walking with me, just the two of us. It was the last walk we ever went on, and he knelt down on the ground near our house and scooped dirt into his hands. He let the dirt whisper through his fingers into my hand. *'This is your land. This land, it is in your blood, and in your heart. No matter where you travel, this land, it is always in you. Remember that, and you will never be far from home.'* And all those months later, all alone and further away than ever, I remembered my abbi's words. I picked up the dirt on the new ground I walked, I scooped with both of my hands just like Abbi had, and let that dirt fall through my fingers just the same. I tried to feel it. I tried to remember.

But now I get it, what my abbi was saying, what Miran was trying to get me to understand all those years he whispered his Tomorrow Stories and talked of home. It's not our old home he was telling. It's the home that will be. Home will be wherever we make it. Wherever we remember who we are. And just like that, standing in the drain, with those candles burning and Riverman watching, I understand, I remember.

I remember my ummi and my abbi and my brother and my teta and my aunts and cousins and uncles. I remember them all, whole and full and alive, and I feel that feeling which I'd forgotten even existed, telling me my family is all around me, with me. And I know stronger than ever now that I'll never let them be forgotten again. I'll soar their souls from my tongue, and build back all they cared for and tell of all they loved.

I understand then, more than ever, that free is free from fear and I've been running too long. I haven't let myself remember, so my heart wouldn't burn. But I'm ready now. I am the speaker for my dead, and I will find my home.

Riverman stares those river rock eyes right into my bones. He starts talking at me in those almost words of his, and then his words turn to animal, to a music, pouring into my ears in pictures and colours and feelings that rush over me until the only thing I am seeing is Riverman's song. Miran and Isa and Skeet and me following Riverman along the river, through the forests and seas, walking on and on until we're at our beach, with our country growing up around us, whole and strong. And I'm there with that golden sand and warm, warm water. There are no bodies, and no sadness, just a sureness washing in with every wave. I can hear the wind whispering the leaves and Skeet whistling in my ears and his arm is around my shoulder and I'm smiling at him and Miran is laughing and Isa is splashing and playing and our birds are flying around us and the sun is beating down warm and everywhere is a feeling of safe and wholeness and a knowing that we never have to run, not ever again. We are free.

When Riverman stops singing, I look to Skeet, and he's got tears tracking down his face too. I wonder if he saw the same dream I did, or if his promise was different. Isa is curled up against the wall, and there is a bright burning right off him the same way it burns off all those people and all those birds in the picture behind him. It's almost as though Isa has become part of the picture, like he is there, having his soul lifted by the strange woman in the middle.

Riverman reaches out and take hold of my wrist. He looks at the snake. Then he takes his finger and traces it along my arm. Along the tattoo. He looks at me and I see my pain aching in those silvered eyes of his. He reaches to the shelf, and takes hold of a piece of rock, dark black and glinting in the candlelight. Then he holds my wrist gently in his own and starts scratching at my skin.

There's a pain, edging up at me from the lines he draws, but it's a good pain, a sharp leaking out all the hurt from my body. Isa is looking over his shoulder as he does it, a smile growing on his face as he watches. 'Oh Esra,' he says.

I don't look. Not until Riverman is done. Then I hold my arm up to a candle, and that snake, curling up from my arm has been turned to the tail and body of a fox. My fox, with his torn up ear, stepping gently along my arm, listening to the beating of my heart and the whispering of my soul. And that tattoo no longer tells of the Snakeskins owning me, of being lost and stolen and disappeared and forgotten. It tells of a strong and the promise of free. And instead of the letters *OP*, Riverman has added an H at the top and an E at the bottom, and I hear Isa whispering the word. 'HOPE,' he reads.

And suddenly I hear Miran's voice in my head and remember that last riddle he told, right before the fire. '*I am always there, but no one can see me. I can be held on to, but never touched. If you lose me, nothing will matter. What am I?*' I can't wait to tell him. I get it now.

Riverman smiles and grunts again, his finger tracing down my cheek.

'Esra,' Isa says, and he's standing next to me, looking at something on the very edge of the shelf. It's a piece of material, torn and tied into a knot around a bright, white feather. I finger the knot in my own shirt. 'Miran.'

Riverman nods and puts his hand to the bracelet around my wrist. 'Where is he? Take me to him. Please.'

Riverman's eyes twist to the back of his head, and he grunts then turns Miran's knot over in my hand. There's something there, printed on the fabric. It's a dragon, blue, with a sword sticking from its back.

'I've seen that,' Skeet says. 'I've seen it before, but I can't think . . . St George and the Dragon!' And his face brights up. 'That's the dragon! Don't you see? He's at the hospital – St George's hospital! That's it isn't it?'

Riverman is sitting on the floor now, watching the shadows flickering the walls. He doesn't move. I touch his arm. 'Will you come with us? To find Miran? To start living?'

Riverman looks at me, and back at the wall. 'Will you?' I ask again. He takes my hand in his and points back out the drain, and we turn, as if Miran would be waiting for us at the top of the steps. There's nothing there though. Just the black of the drain, deeper now from inside the candlelit room.

Riverman turns his head, slowly to the side. He listens, and his face is so hard now I can see where the mud is cracking along his check.

That's when we hear it. A thundering. Riverman throws his hands to his ears and his head shakes faster and faster, the fear splintering off him. He looks at me. His eyes burning the river right at me. He pulls my knife from his pocket and he puts it in my hand, squeezing my fingers tight around the handle.

We can hear the water, the thundering, the roaring. Isa is gripping my arm, his eyes clenched shut and that noise tears through the tunnel, setting the walls shivering and our ears echoing. And just like that, all at once, every single candle in the room blows out.

Skeet

I never did turn my torch off. It's the only thing left lighting up the room when every one of those candles blows out. I grab the torch and grab Isa, and Esra's grabbed me, and we're spinning around the room but the Riverman's gone, totally up and vanished like he was never even here at all. And just when we need him to get us out of here. Useless as an ashtray on a motorbike.

The roof explodes then, with all them birds and bats, and they're screeching and calling and flapping about our heads and I don't give a damn how clever and brave Esra reckons pigeons are, I never did like the buggers and now they're making everything harder and scarier, with their wings crashing at us and all of them flapping to get away. They've at least wings to get away on.

We run. The water is fighting us, getting higher and stronger and faster and angrier, roaring all around us and thundering like an army of horses. We're down the stairs and into the drain pushing against the water, until we're back at the archway leading to *HELL* and there's still no sign of Riverman.

We look up the tunnel leading back to Em's camp. It's like looking into the mouth of a bleeding river.

'We can't go back that way,' I yell over the water. 'We'll never be able to push against the water.'

We hold each other close, all three of us, and we turn down the tunnel to *HELL*, trying not to turn soft and cry like babes for our mams. Trying to find a way out.

Esra

The water is getting stronger. Angry and pushing at our legs, trying to trip us over and under. 'Stay close to the walls,' Skeet tells us. A rat floating past grabs on to me and scuts up my arm and over my head and on to a ledge in the tunnel wall. If only we could do the same. Skeet shines his light on the rat and the rat looks straight back at me. His tail waves circles in the air keeping balanced up there on that ledge. He looks at me, then turns and balances along that ledge into the dark, following the water rushing beneath him. I watch his shadow, big and fierce running along the drain behind him.

'He'll be heading for a way out.' My voice barely makes it over the rush of the water. But Skeet nods and somehow we manage to push ourselves along the same tunnel the rat turned down, Isa between us and hanging on to the two of us to stop himself being swept away, holding us all together.

We go slower now, all three of us holding each other, the water pushing us harder and faster, our fingers trying to keep grip on the slimed walls. The water is over my waist now and Isa is riding my back to keep from going under. We turn a corner and the air from outside slams into us. I can see the night outside, beautiful and black and shining the moon straight at us. The rat is sat, perched on the edge of the drain, waiting for us, watching to see we made it. For a moment, I feel strong and sure, feeling that wind on my face and knowing we've found the night.

But only for a moment. Because that night is blocked by a metal grill, a padlock the size of my fist stopping us from pushing free. My body slams the grill and the water rises around us, pushing over my shoulders now, and Isa is climbing, trying to suck air into his little lungs. From the other side of the grill the rat twitches his nose.

And then, floating over all the noise of the water and the storming outside, I hear it. A song, sung to me so long ago I didn't even think to remember it. But as soon as I hear it, I know just what it is, just what it means. It's a song Miran used to sing to his pigeons. He taught it to me years back so I'd know it when he gave me my baby pigeon to train. It's Miran. He's singing. He's alive, somewhere down that tunnel, singing his song down to me, and I listen to that song and let my mind fly free on the music pouring into my ears.

Miran is alive. I hope he finds his way home.

I watch as the rat turns once on the ledge and looks right at me. Then he jumps out and into the night.

Miran

Miran wakes. He is back in his bed. He feels as though his sleep had been merely seconds. He wonders what woke him. There is a smell, of dark wet earth in his room, and a faint keening rising up towards him. He searches for his bird, but the window shows nothing but a deep black. Outside his room is the soft light of the hallway at night. He can see the policeman, sitting in his chair, sipping from a cup. He hears a nurse talking softly as she passes by, and he wonders how long it is until they come back to check on him. He thinks of calling out, of pressing a button, of making them come, but everything feels so difficult. He realises he doesn't really care any more.

'Are you there?' He doesn't know if he says the words out loud, or merely thinks them, but still he waits for Death to respond. There is a sound of water rushing from the drain, getting louder, angrier. The river is rising up again, he thinks. It's rising up to take me home. He thinks of Esra, of her smile, and their

promise. He hopes with everything in him that she has found her way home. He thinks of little Isa. Tears of a bull will set you free, *he thinks. He hopes Isa remembers. He hopes Isa holds on to that truth until he too finds his happiness. Miran can feel his body drifting. He has become nothing more than a shadow. He looks one last time for his bird in the dark, but he is not there. Miran wonders if he ever really was.*

His head is on fire, his body burning hot, and yet he feels chilled as well, as though he is being dunked in buckets of ice. From somewhere in the back of his mind, words start to form. 'A long time ago, in a place long forgotten . . .' But there is nothing more to say, and Miran realises he has no more tales to tell. So he whispers the only thing that feels true, his cracked and tired voice barely audible. 'The end.'

Miran's heart struggles to find the strength to continue to beat, his lungs sucking smaller and smaller amounts of air through his body. Soon his body will go into shock and he will start to seizure, his lungs will stop working, and his heart will stop beating. But Miran does not know this, nor does he care.

He closes his eyes. Feathers brush soft against his forehead, and he feels the gentle of a pigeon rubbing his cheek. He hears a soft coo. It is singing, a song about riding the wind and following the rivers. A song of coming home.

Miran's wings push against the cold hard cement,

lifting him higher and higher. He follows the white of his pigeon through the dark, to the small window opening onto the street and out into the orange pulse of the cool night air. All around, he can feel the bodies of one hundred birds push in close, keeping him warm, their gentle thrumming hushing him. His head is filled with countless tales, shaping his spirit, setting his soul soaring. 'They can take everything, but they can never take our stories . . .' He thinks of feathers and wind and rocks and the sea. His flock gather around him, carrying him further away from the pain and sadness, until the small, broken body lying in the bed is little more than a distant memory.

Outside, not too far away, just the other side of the town, an explosion of birds and bats erupts from a manhole on the main street. They tumble from the dark depths up into the sky, a tornado of wings beating in time. Anyone looking would have thought this was a sign of some sort. But the night is too dark and stormy for anyone to see a thing.

Skeet

The water is pushing us harder against that grill. Slamming into us fast as blazes. I guess this is what the sign meant. *HELL* it is then. And even though I'm right pissed off with my mam and dad, I can't help thinking that it really is shocking bad luck. I mean, jeeez. What are the chances of having two kids just to see them both drown to their deaths. Maybe they're cursed. Maybe they were both real bad people in their past lives, like mass murderers or something. Seems hardly fair that Pauly and me are the ones that end up paying for it, but I guess there have to be sacrifices. Maybe this is just to serve them right for being such crap parents in this life. I hope they cry their damn eyes out.

I can't see a way out any more. Even if we wanted to, we couldn't fight our way backwards against that water. Even Croakus is jumping around like crazy in my pocket, and that damn toad can breathe under water. Must be he's worried about me, bless the little fella. We're holding on and trying to breathe in the air through the grill but the water is coming so hard and fast that it's near impossible not to choke on it. It's coming in waves over our heads and I can see the rain still bucketing down outside.

That damn rat fooled us. I take Croakus from my pocket. There's no time for long goodbyes. Even still, he gives me the kind of grunt which means I'm the damned best owner a toad could wish for, and he'll miss me. 'Save yourself!' I tell him, and push him through the grill and down into the river. He doesn't argue.

The water is rushing harder against me, pushing the last bit of air out of my lungs. I've been holding on to Isa but now my fingers can't hold on any more and I'm under.

There's no light this time. No brother to save me. I feel my body smash against the floor of the drain. I can't hold my breath any longer. I let my eyes close and my body turns floppy and soft. I see those river spirits from my dreams swimming towards me, fighting their way up the drains to get to me, their sharp little teeth gnashing sharp and smiling, all evil just like Mam said they were. I see Mam, clear as day. She's down by the river in the dark of the night, nothing on but her dressing gown and the pink fluffy bunny slippers I bought her for her birthday, her body shaking from the fear of being out in the dark and wet. She's down there though, looking for something. I can see her eyes all close, searching, and she's calling something, over and over. Then she sees my green scarf, wash past her in the river. And in my dream, I watch as my mam takes a deep breath. She's reaching for that scarf. She takes a step into the river. She's watching that water race over her foot. She calls out again. Then she takes another step into the river, and I hear them river spirits that stole my brother screeching and laughing, and everything goes dark.

Esra

Skeet goes under. I call out, my hands pushing to find him, but there's only the water pushing at me, fast and furious and too, too high. My fingers lose their grip on the grill, and the water takes me. My body smashes against the grill. I look for Miran dancing, for the light and dream that Skeet talked of, but there is only black. My chest aches with the heavy of holding on. My legs stop their kicking. They know when to give up, when the red hot fire of living is only something remembered. My mouth opens and mudded water fills my lungs.

I can taste Riverman, the rot and clay and fur, seeping into me, his smell, stronger than ever, flowing through me, turning me into river, and his hands, slippery and slick, pulling me down deeper.

From somewhere far away, I hear my fox screaming into the night. I think of the soft of my brother's fingers wrapping my hand and the smell of jasmines picked fresh from the grass. I hear my teta's voice, clear and bright, and feel the warm embrace of my parents. They are dancing in the kitchen, but this time I am with them, their arms holding me tight between them, and I can hear the music we are all dancing to.

Then everything turns to black and there's nothing left of the world but thick dark mud, burying me down deep, right to the very soul of the earth.

Skeet

I'm back in that dream the Riverman sang to me in the chamber. This must be the way to heaven I'm guessing. Following the dream. I can hear the water crashing about me still, feel the cold of it, and the ache of every part of my body, and I know as sure as my name is Skeet O'Malley that I'm as dead as a donkey's donger. I said there was no escaping those drains when it rains. But no one ever listens, oh no.

I keep following the dream Riverman sang. It's me and Mam by the river, our toes tickling the water and my mam laughing the way she used to. Back when she would hold my hand in hers and we would walk together, our arms swinging back and forth and her smile . . . I hold on to that dream and wait for heaven to open its doors.

My mam's singing is so strong in the dream, and her hand so real, brushing the hair from my eyes, over and over like she used to when I was a little one. I feel her lips brush my eyelids, and her fingers wiping my face and I can feel her tears falling warm on my cheeks.

And suddenly, I can open my eyes. But it's not heaven, and it's not the dream. It's very early morning and I'm on the bank of the river and Mam is there. Soaked through in her dressing gown and fluffy bunny slippers and holding my body in hers and rocking it back and forth. It's not just any bank of river we're on neither. This here, this was right where Pauly and me went swimming that day. I wonder if that was why Mam came down here, in her dressing gown and all. If she came for Pauly, or if she came for me.

I'm covered head to toe in mud, and when I move I can feel the mud cracking open against my skin like I'm breaking out from a shell. Riverman must be close too, because I can smell him, stronger than ever, and lying just behind me, her eyes open and watching and alive is Esra, with little Isa wrapped in her arms and holding to her neck. They smile at me, bigger smiles than I've ever seen.

Mam sees my eyes open and she's screaming and kissing me and telling me sorry, and promising that things'll be different now and how she'll get help, for real this time, she'll book herself into a clinic and go to all the meetings for the rest of her life, and never, ever go back to the way things were before. Then she stares me right in the eye and says how lucky she is to be my mam.

'It was the strangest thing,' she says then, and her

eyes go all cloudy, 'but when that storm started raging, I heard something calling me or something. Like this voice I'd never heard before, but it sounded real familiar, and it was calling and calling and I opened the door and saw the rain, and all of a sudden I knew where you'd gone. I knew this was where I'd find you. Down here in the dark and the wet. I knew this was where you'd be. And when I saw your scarf in the water, I thought . . . I thought I'd lost you too.' Mam looks back at me then and she's not smiling, but she's seeing me. Really seeing me.

'I love you, Skeet,' she says. 'More than anything in the whole world, and I'm so, so very sorry I ever let you forget it.' And even though I'm too big for it now, I bury my head in Mam's shoulders and start crying for all I'm worth.

'I know, Mam,' I tell her. 'I love you, too.'

A pigeon drops from the sky then, settling itself on top of crashed over tree. Mam points at it and says, 'Look, Skeet. You know your gran used to race pigeons. Big beautiful white ones like that one, she did. I've never liked birds much myself, but she loved them.'

'Ah Mam,' I tell her. 'Pigeons are all right. They're real smart you know. They can read the alphabet and remember faces, and are brave and everything. I've always loved pigeons, I have.'

I hear Esra snort behind me. Rude.

'Well then,' she says, 'perhaps I should give them

Esra

I'm not dead. Somehow I'm still alive, mud covering every part of me like a second skin. I feel the crack of mud along my face and I lie in the sun and watch Skeet curled into his Mam, and the look on his face is happiness, whole and simple.

I think of the water, the river, the drain and the dark, and I pull Isa into me, breathing him in. That river, so calm now, could have taken us all. *And the river will lead us home.*

Isa's taking in the sun, just starting to spread its warm over the earth and he smiles at me, that same smile he had when he looked into his fire. Like he's seen what's to come and is ready for it.

It's then I see the pocket watch in my hand. The glass broken and dripping. Riverman's watch. His heart and soul. But I can feel the beat in my hand. The watch is ticking.

I feel my tears fall on Isa's head, sliming a path down the mud on my face. He looks at me and rubs the mud from my wrist. We both stare a long while at the fox still burning bright right back at us.

'Suck it up, princess. We're not dead yet,' Isa says. 'We can go to Miran now, then follow Riverman home,' and there is so much hope in him that I can't bear to show him the pocket watch held in my hand, or to point to the old raincoat, crumpled and caught in the roots of a tree, with no living left in it at all.

Skeet

'Skeet.' It's Esra, she's kneeling next to me, not looking at Mam, just staring right into my eyes. 'You stay, but—'

'But nothing,' I tell her back, right off. If she thinks I've come this far just to pull out now because my Mam's here, then she's neuro-diverser than I thought. Mam pulls me into her again. She doesn't try to stop me getting up though. She knows.

'I've something to do, Mam. Something that needs to be done.' Mam looks at me and nods, and even though she starts up her crying again, she says, 'I know you do. Just, Skeet, I'll be here. I'll be waiting for you when you're done. If you need me, like.'

And even though I thought I'd never, not ever go into a drain again, that's straight where we're headed. Because we've all of us spotted the drain whooshing its water into the river. And we've all seen the brown hand print, mosaicked from broken glass, waving us into the dark of the drain, and a white pigeon pieced together to fly from the hand like it's finally been set free. It's white, with bits of grey in its tail, just like the one Mam and I were looking at.

Mam watches as we go, her hand at her mouth. We look at the sky and hope like hell, but there's never been a bluer sky, without even a single cloud in it, like the storm came and washed the sky and everything in the whole world cleaner than it's ever been.

We step into the drain, and we can already see another bird flashing to us further along. It's a whole trail of them we're following. Like the fairy tale where the kids follow the breadcrumbs home, we're following those birds.

A lump and an ache grows in my throat then, thinking that he's not ever making another picture, or singing another song to us again. Esra showed me the pocket watch. I know she was thinking the same thing as me. That those hands ticking on the watch were like hands waving goodbye.

We're running now to get to Miran, tripping over everything that the storm's sucked down into these drains. If we weren't in such a hurry I'd stop and start collecting. There's a whole heap of stuff down here. Most of it is broken, but a whole lot could be fixed up into something else. I've stepped over about ten footballs, a broken radio and even a bike with a wheel only a little bit bent. I stopped just a second to check out the wheel. There was something caught on the handlebars. In the dark I thought it might be Croakus come back to find me. It wasn't. It was just an old rubber duck made to look like Shakespeare with a stupid little beard and a piece of paper saying *To Quack or Not to Quack*. I pulled the duck out from the handlebars and put it back in the water. It floated off happily, making its way back to the river. For a second there, I thought it winked at me as it floated away.

We're running faster now, our legs pushing through the water, our muscles aching, but those birds keep leading us, further and further through the drains. We turn a corner and it's not a bird now, but another of the big Riverman pictures, just like the ones in his lair. I put my hand on top of his mudded up signature of a handprint and try to feel him still alive somehow.

But Esra's not looking at the handprint. She's stopped dead, staring at the picture, her eyes wider than I've ever seen. The picture is a room all full up of plants that curl from the picture into these vines that are growing right up the tunnel wall. I touch them, just to make sure they're really real 'cause I don't know how anything can grow in this dark. And in between the plants, there's a kid lying and broken and all in bits like pieces of a puzzle not put together. There's another kid, curled up into a ball, and then one last kid, all broken up too, but this one's standing and holding a baseball bat. And right by this one's feet is the horriblest monster I've ever seen. That picture'll give me nightmares for weeks, I can tell you now.

That monster is all hairy and huge, with fangs dripping with blood and eyes all angry and claws that could take your arm right off of you. But the kid with the bat is stood over it, and you can tell from looking that the monster is dead, all blooded up, the marks of the bat still on it. And all around the picture, in the dark, are eyes, just eyes, staring and watching. The whole thing gives me shivers right up my back all the way to the very top of my skull, and when you look real close at the picture, you can see where that monster's blood has turned to real and is dripping right out of that wall and puddling in rusted red on the floor.

Esra cries out, her legs drop right out from under her and she starts up screaming, but with not so much as a sound coming from her mouth. She's rocking back and forth, her arms wrapped around herself.

Isa runs to her and holds her and there's fear all over his little face. 'Help her, Skeet, you've got to help her!' And I get it then. I understand. That kid with the bat, that there is the part of Esra's story she left out, been pulled by Riverman right from her head and breathing out of these walls straight at us.

Isa is holding her face in his hands. 'You had to do it, Esra. You had to save us. It's not true what he said. You're nothing like him. Esra. Listen. There's only one monster in the picture. Only one.'

I pick up Esra's arm in my hand and twist her wrist so she's looking at Riverman's tattoo. 'Look at the fox,

Esra Merkes. Look at it. That's who you are. You are Esra Merkes and you're going to find Miran. Just like you said you would.'

Esra puts her hand over the fox and closes her eyes and breathes in deep and long. When her eyes open again, she stands up and looks again at the picture. She breathes it in. But there's a strength to her now. This time, she's owning it.

'There's another bird,' she says then. That bird is stopped right on the edge of the picture, but turned looking at us. Esra moves up close to look in those bird's eyes, and something happens. Looking at her I reckon she's growing taller and stronger right there in front of us. She nods then and looks at me. 'Come on then,' she says, like I was the one holding everyone up.

We start running again, following the birds flashing us from the bricks, and then just like that the tunnel comes to a stop. One last bird is etched into the wall, sitting this time, looking up at the roof of the drain. Esra and Isa and me follow its stare, right up to a grill, all greased and black. There's a white light shining through the grill and lighting up the water of the drain.

Esra shines her torch straight up through that grill, and I swear, a bird as white as the bird from the pictures takes off from the other side of the grill and disappears out of the way of the torch. Esra pushes me down and climbs on to my back, pushing up at the grill with all that's in her. The grill pops off and she pulls herself up and out of the drain. And then all I can hear is crying and calling from Esra, and Isa is scrambling, trying to get through. I push him up and try to shimmy on up the walls of the drain. It only takes a couple of goes, and then Esra is there, grabbing my arm and pulling me through.

Her eyes are all shaky though, and it doesn't take even a second for me to see why. There he is. Miran.

Miran's having a fit of some kind, his whole body jerking until he suddenly stops and lies still, all limp. He isn't moving, not even with Isa shaking him and holding his head and crying and begging and all.

I crawl over and feel for a pulse, check for his breathing. But there's nothing. Not even a little thump, and looking at him lying there like that all I can see is Silviu's face staring back at me. 'Esra—'

But Esra shakes her head and pushes me back and starts on doing some kind of strange CPR, except she's doing it all wrong. Everyone knows that's not how you do it. I don't bother explaining, don't waste any more time, just push her out of the way and start on him myself.

I don't expect nothing to happen. But I'm not doing it for Miran. I'm doing it for Isa. I'm doing it for Esra. Esra runs for the door, screaming at the very top of her lungs. Alarms start popping off every which way, and nurses and doctors are flooding in. Those doctors take one look at me and Miran and shove me out of the way without so much as a thank you very much.

But as they start to wheel him out on the bed, I hear them. 'He's breathing and there's a faint pulse.' I don't hear the rest of what they say. Because I did it. He was dead and I made him alive again. Just like I brought Riverman to life. I've gone and brought the dead to life and all. Me. I knew I'd be good at CPR. I think maybe when I grow up, if I don't decide to join the circus, I think maybe I'll be a doctor.

Then I see the words on the door. *Overflow Room 1.* Just like Silviu had figured. There's a chair outside the door too, but its empty, and now that *P. Guard* makes sense and all. Trust the bleeding police to be gone right when you need their help.

Esra is still shaking, but smiling now too, and we're holding each other and rocking back and forward while everything is going crazy all around us and sirens are sounding and people are running and staring into the drain with their torches and there are guards and doctors and nurses, and now the bloody useless policeman is back and trying to look in control and they're all talking at us and pulling on us and us three are just holding tight.

Over all that noise, I hear it. A slapping of wings. I look up, and there's the pigeon, bright white with grey specks all on its tail, flying out of a window and into the sky.

Esra

They let us stay, waiting for Miran in his room. A nurse came with dry clothes for all of us, and plastic sandals for our feet. But Isa wouldn't give up his shoes, and when she reached for mine, I shook my head.

'You can't go around just taking someone's shoes!' Skeet said, and looked so shocked that the nurse backed away.

They explained how Miran had been poisoned. 'You found him just in time. By the sounds of it, he was officially dead for about a minute there. Well done, you kids. You saved him.' They explained how they were flushing him out now, and that as soon as they had he would start to feel better, but he would need a lot of time for his body to rest and recover. And when they wheeled him back in, tubes up his nose, and sleeping, I cried out with the happiness of seeing him alive.

They wanted us to leave then. But Skeet started up shouting how his uncle is the best lawyer in the whole city and they would regret this for the rest of their days if they even thought about keeping us apart, and didn't they know we were just kids who were already traumatised, and that if they did anything else to traumatise us more they'd be paying for it for the rest of their sorry little lives, and that we should be able to do anything we god damn wanted because we were heroes and the newspapers would love to hear about how they were treating us.

I guess they just wanted Skeet to shut up, because they waved their hands in the air and told him all right, Isa and me could sit by Miran's bed, but that we couldn't wake him or cause any fuss or we'd be out. They kept the policeman outside the room as well. A different policeman to the one from before.

But nothing else matters now. Not now I'm with Miran. I tied his bracelet back around his wrist and Whispered Tomorrows deep into his ear. He didn't wake up, but he could hear me. I know because when I told him all about the circus we were going to start, his fingers squeezed mine, promising. He slept a long time. I did too, Isa curled at his feet, and when I woke up into Miran's brown eyes smiling at me, a happiness pushed through me so strong it nearly swept me away. I felt his fingers pull at the knot in my shirt, trying to untie it, but it wouldn't budge. I guess it had been there too long.

'Hope,' I tell him. 'The answer to your stupid riddle. It's hope.'

Miran's smile grows even bigger. 'Took you long enough,' he says.

We started laughing then, our tears choking us both until a nurse came and told us to settle down. She said it with a smile though, and brought us all in some food. She took the tubes from Miran's nose and checked his breathing and let me listen to his heart beating and she wrote all of everything down in his chart. 'You'll be better before you know it,' she told him.

'Did you catch them? The person who poisoned him?'

The nurse looked at me and told me that was a matter for police. She turned to go, then looked back at us. 'But no. I don't think they have. Not yet anyhow. But don't you worry. You're all quite safe now.'

Miran waited until the nurse left. 'That's what she said before. Soon as we can, we're out of here. We're going home.' Miran looks at Isa and smiles. Isa smiles back.

I don't tell him that I'm not going home. That I can't. He needs to rest up a bit more before I tell him that. He needs to get just a little stronger. Even thinking it, I know I'm just buying us some time together. But I watch him settle back in his bed and I promise, whatever happens, whatever Tomorrow turns out to be, I won't ever forget.

I could have sat there in that room for ever, I reckon. I look at Miran and I keep buying time. More time than

I should. Telling myself that Miran is too weak to tell, that it will make him worse. But I have to tell him now, before they move us out, before the police get in first. I want to do this the right way. I won't be cornered. I won't be trapped.

I put my hand over Miran's. He takes a long, slow drink, his eyes burning with the knowing of what's to come.

'Do you remember that girl?' I whisper. I don't need to say any more. There was only ever one 'that girl'.

'She got away,' Miran's voice is almost too soft to hear right. Almost.

'How long did she last running?' I say. 'Three weeks? Not even? And do you remember how we all said she'd come back to save us? That she'd have gone for help, remember? And how even in all our hoping we knew it wasn't true. We knew she'd be running as fast and furious and as far away as she could.'

'And we hated her for it,' Miran finishes, and his voice is as cracked and croaked as mine.

'When they caught her—'

Miran shakes his head and puts his hands to his ears. Isa is crying, big heavy tears that fall to the sheets and spread in dark circles. I pull Miran's hands from his ears. 'Remember,' I say, but this time it isn't a question. This time, I am the one pulling the memory from the dark and blooming it to life. 'When they caught her, we all said it served her right. We all said she deserved it, for not coming back for us. But we knew, Miran. And we hated her because she failed. She didn't make it. She was our promise and she failed.'

Miran looks at me. His fingers touch my face, and then reach down and trace over the fox burning bright in black on my wrist. I hold his hand against my head. 'It's all in here, Miran. And maybe, maybe it won't do a single thing of good. Maybe they won't listen. But maybe they will. Maybe it will stop someone else from getting in that truck. Just one person maybe. And maybe that's OK.'

Miran is crying, silent streams mapping his face. I want to tell Miran that I am the speaker for my dead, but I am the speaker for the living too. Of all those lost and forgotten and disappeared, whose tongues can't tell. But I don't. Instead, I kiss his fingers.

'It was me that hit him. Me that killed him. You don't need to be there, Miran. You go. Find your home and your free with Isa. Find your birds. Follow the river and get to the beach, just like you said. And later, I'll come find you.' I mean it too, every word. If I go on running, I won't ever be free. But Miran, he's as brave and beautiful and more full of hope than anyone. Miran, he needs to finish his dream.

'Free is us, together, Esra. Always was, always will be.' Miran pulls Isa closer to him. 'We'll get to the beach. Just might take longer is all,' Miran doesn't look scared either.

I look at the policeman waiting outside. Skeet's been out there with him for ages, chattering on to him, and from the look on the cop's face he's getting ready to tell him to get. Poor guy doesn't know what he's in for.

'Should I call in the copper? We can tell him all of everything here,' I say.

'I hate the police,' Miran says back. 'And Esra, there's something I want to see before we do. I want to see the moon. I want to sit on the grass and taste the night and look up at that moon again. I want you to sing me that old song you used to sing, do you remember?' I had forgotten I had ever sung that song to Miran, forgotten it had ever left my lips.

'Esra?' Isa looks at me. He's holding the card Silviu tried to give me. The one with the name of the police sergeant on it. I didn't know Isa had kept it. I wonder if he was planning to use it himself. Little Isa, he's more grown up now than I ever thought. 'Let's use the good one, Esra, like Silviu said. The one who listens.'

Isa and me help Miran out of the bed. It is dark night outside, but there are still lights on in the hallways and the policeman guarding us in.

Skeet turns to us then, his Grandda Tom's sixth sense whispering to him just like he says it does. He looks at me and nods.

'Get ready,' I say to Miran.

'I'm always ready,' he says back, even though just standing is causing him more hurt than I could think to imagine.

We watch Skeet arguing with the policeman, who's puffing himself up and pointing now, and Skeet is puffing himself up and pointing right back. Then Skeet makes a grab for his hat, grabbing a chunk of the poor man's hair too, and before he's even worked out what's happened, Skeet's off down the hallway with the police chasing behind.

It won't take him long to work out what's going on. Won't take long to work out he's been fooled by a little bit of a boy with more strong in him than most people will ever have in their whole lives.

Miran wraps around my shoulder and the three of us leave that place, Miran aching and slow with his body all broken like it is, his leg dragging the cast behind him like Riverman with his wooden leg. But we do it. We drag ourselves out of that room and down those clean, cold stairs and into the dead dark of night.

Together.

We meet Skeet down by our cave. He comes whistling around the corner with a police hat sitting proud on his head and his back turned to us. 'Are you cave kids dressed?' he says, his hand over his eyes. ''Cause in polite society, people don't go around with no clothes on, you know.'

'We're not cave kids,' Miran says back, but Isa and I are too busy laughing to say a thing.

Skeet spins around. He's holding a chocolate cake with *Happy Birthday Granny* written in white icing on the top. 'They didn't want it,' he says, finger scooping cake into his mouth. 'If they wanted it so bad, they wouldn't have left it on the bench by the door for flies to get on, or grubby little kids to stick their fingers in. I bet they made a mistake with the writing and were trying to sell it for cheap. Anyhow, a cake is meant to make people happy, right? And that's what this cake is doing right now. Growing happiness. I mean, hell. If anyone deserves a bit of happy it's us, isn't it? After all we've been through? And I don't see you helping out on the whole feeding us front. You could try and carry your weight a bit more if you know what I mean, because so far you haven't brought much to the whole operation.'

Skeet smiles at me, and takes a bottle of red fizz from his pocket. 'Raspberry lemonade?' he offers.

I take the bottle. 'The perfect accompaniment to any meal,' I say back, and close my eyes, letting the fizz play on my tongue, and telling my brain to remember this. Right now.

We sit for a long time then, Isa in the middle and no one saying a word. Not even Skeet. Isa moves around so he's curled up on Miran, holding tight to his shirt and sucking away at his sleeve like always. I can tell how much pain it's giving Miran, but he doesn't let on, just smiles his big smile down at Isa. That smile with a thousand promises wrapped inside.

'*What gets wetter the more it dries?*' Miran says then, and groans when I shove him in the side.

'No more riddles. Please,' I tell him. Beside me, I can hear Skeet, saying the riddle to himself over and over again.

'I give up. What?' Skeet says.

'There's no giving up,' Miran says back, and I laugh at the look on Skeet's face.

My fingers find Miran's and they squeeze. The fingers on my other hand find Skeet's fingers and they squeeze, too. Skeet squeezes back, so hard that I feel my fingers crumpling from the pressure of it and the pain is bursting at me to call out. I don't though. Damn boy doesn't even know how to squeeze right.

'Skeet.' I look at him. He turns away, knowing at what's coming. 'We need to go to the police station,' I tell him. He shakes his head and sniffs.

'You don't have to do a damn thing.' But he knows, he understands, and after a bit he stands up, hands on hips and chin pushed forward. 'Well, come on then. I don't have time to waste showing people all around town you know. I've got more important things to do.' He's crying when he says it.

He waits until Miran and Isa are turned, then Skeet scoops a handful of water from the river and pours it into my hands. 'You made him, just as much as me. He's in your blood now. And so am I. Family. This here is part of you now. Don't forget it.' And that water dripping through my hands mixes with the dirt my abbi poured into my hands so many years ago, mixing and turning in my soul, and filling me with a deep and heavy peace, and when I look at the water in my hands, all that's left is a small puddle of mud. I squeeze my hand around that mud, and stamp it strong on Skeet's chest. Skeet looks at my mudded up hand print stamped on him and nods.

We follow the river back towards town, Skeet whistling my teta's moon song. Isa stops once, and turns back to face the wild. He tugs at my hand. 'Do you see them?' he asks. I look to the faded light of the night, at the fog rising up from the darkness of the river, and I do. I see them. He's there, Riverman, his shadow dancing along behind us, tall and strong, and not a speck of hurt on him. And right next to him, holding his hand, and wearing a pair of binoculars around his neck, is Silviu.

A smile spreads across my face and wet pricks at my eyes. 'I knew you could,' Isa says. He kisses my hand and skips to catch up with Miran, and I feel the tick of Riverman's watch against my chest, beating right in time with the ticking of my own heart.

I breathe the air deep, remembering the feel of the cold, the wet, the promise of it. There's a smell, thick on the wind, of seaweed and mud. Skeet stops and turns around and stares into the dark. 'Do you smell that?' he whispers. I nod and breathe that smell in deep.

By the time we reach the police station, the dark is already fading from the sky. Skeet points to a drain at the edge of the road. 'Do you think anyone is there? Right now? Under us? We could go back you know. Find the mole kids and live under there and—'

I reach out for Skeet's hands and hold them tight in my own. 'We'll go back. Someday. Back to the heart of the river. Back to his room and all he collected. Back to those doors with the music and laughing. We might even find some mole kids or skeletons or even some treasure,' and I smile at Skeet.

'We already found the treasure, Marble Brains,' he says back, turning his face from the drain to look me in the eye. 'The first thing you do is ask for that copper on the card. That one. No one else. You got that? Don't say a word to anyone else, you hear me, Esra Merkes? Because you've got marbles for brains but I know about these things. I've seen it a million times on TV, and you've got to get the good one, and—' Skeet's crying now and pulling at my arm. 'Don't do it. You don't have to. You don't need to tell anyone. Please Esra.' He stops, and his voice is just a whisper, barely there: 'Don't leave me.'

And now my throat is choking up. 'Skeet,' but his head keeps shaking and his hands fly to his ears to shoo away my words. I take his hand in mine and bring it to my lips. 'We weren't the only ones, Skeet. There are lots of us. Hidden away and disappeared. Miran and Isa and me, we're the lucky ones. Those other kids are still kept. No one sees them, no one wants to see them, but they're there – in the nail bars and the farms and restaurants, and cleaning people's houses and stealing on the streets and . . . and I see them. I can help them. I know where they are. I know where Orlando is. I know what the Organ Boys look like good enough to draw them straight, and I know every one of those farms used to keep kids. I know the houses we're kept in. I know what they say to kids and families to fool them to coming. I know it all. I need to do this for every kept kid, for Silviu, and all the other street rats who die in the gutter like that's where they're supposed to be. And if I don't do this now? They won't ever be free. I won't ever be free. I am not theirs any more, Skeet. It was never our doing, that brought us here, no matter what they say. We don't owe Orlando a thing. Not a single one of us. I need to turn that fear wild, Skeet, just like you said.'

'That's just a stupid thing to say. I never said it.' But Skeet grips my hands and holds my eyes tighter than ever. 'Fear's not got nothing on you. Never will. Don't you forget that, Esra Merkes.' Then he pulls me close and wraps his arms around me. I wrap my arms around him right back.

'It was self-defence, you hear? Don't let them say different. You tell them they should give you a medal for what you did. And Esra, after, come find me. Take me to the beach, OK? I've never been to the beach. I want to go. With you. So find me. Show me the sea.'

I nod.

'Do you promise?'

'I promise.' I hold his fingers in mine and squeeze and when he squeezes back, he does it just right.

Isa hugs Skeet. 'See you soon, you big baboon,' Skeet whispers, and turns away so Isa doesn't see the tears trailing his cheeks.

I look back only once. There's a shadow, crouched at the very edge of the wild, waiting, bushed tail and head held high, sniffing the future on the wind, the pads of his feet readying for the thousand journeys to come. I feel the burn of my fox tattoo, and it drags me up, tall and steady. I send my last whisper to my fox, waiting in those trees.

My name is Esra Merkes. I am eleven years old. The tattoo on my arm says I am free. The tattoo on my arm tells of a fierce, wild and strong. I am a speaker for the dead. I am a speaker for the living. I have something to say. And that is my truth.

Miran

It was light when Miran and little Isa and Esra said goodbye to Skeet. The sun was tasting the tops of the buildings and warming the ground at their feet. Skeet waved goodbye to their backs, and watched as they walked into the police station.

Skeet didn't leave though. He wouldn't. He didn't care how long it would take. He wasn't moving until they walked back out, heads held high and free as the bloody birds they kept going on about. And if it took too long, he'd go in there himself and see to it. Those police wouldn't know what hit them.

Inside the police station, Miran and Isa and Esra were shown into a room on the third floor. The room was painted yellow and was full of toys and books and games. Miran and Esra hadn't played with toys or read books for many years. They weren't sure they remembered how. But Isa smiled. He picked up a book, breathing up its smell, his fingers caressing the pictures like they were the most precious things he'd ever laid eyes on.

Esra asked for the name on the card, and the policeman he asked didn't laugh. His eyes weren't blank or tired from knowing. Instead, they were filled with sadness for the children and their busted up bodies standing in front of him. He nodded and went to make the call. He brought them all a cup of hot chocolate and a muffin and asked if there was anyone else they wanted him to phone. He told them Detective Sergeant MacIntyre was on her way.

Miran and Esra sat in the room a long time waiting, watching Isa play and look through those books, his smile full of wonder, and when the door opened, Miran took Esra's fingers in his own. They would be OK.

'Hello,' the woman said. 'My name is Téa. I'm here to help, and listen.' And when no one spoke, the woman sat down on the floor in the middle of the room. 'Take your time. How about I tell you a story first? Come sit with me, and I will tell you the greatest tale you have ever heard, if you wish . . .' Miran lifted his face. There she was. As beautiful as morning, with a voice the colour of the sea and a heart as warm as the summer sun.

Outside, a white pigeon, flecked with grey and with brilliant blue eyes, stood on the windowsill. The pigeon watched the woman inside, as she swirled her stories and tales into the air. The sun moved across the sky, and her smile reached deep inside the three children, until they began to let go of their sadnesses.

Then she sat, and held their hands, and she gentlied the heaviest words from their hearts, until they once again remembered how to hope. The soft orange of a Tomorrow blossomed softly around them, and none of them noticed the pigeon watching from the window, or all the birds of different sizes and colours gathered on the eaves and wires around the building.

The clouds wisped past, and the trees murmured to the wind brushing over the leaves. The songs and stories of the birds coming home filled the air, and the warm of the whole world fell on the woman's cheeks.

There was a whisper of wind and a flutter of wings, and the pigeon took flight. He spun a single circle in the air, feeling the joy of the wind in his feathers and the warmth of the sun on his back, before coming to rest for the very last time on the sill of the window. Neither the woman nor the children noticed his presence. All was as it should be.

Far below, a boy sat on a fence, waiting. He was staring at a picture etched into the bricks of the police station wall, the bone white splinters pulsing with life. It was a picture of a bull, just like the ones in the museum, except this bull had a man's face, old and creased and cracked with mud, and the tears in its eyes were falling down his face and turning to a river by his feet. The boy spent a long time drinking in that picture, and when he touched the tear falling from the bull's eye, his finger came away wet.

'Tears of a bull will set you free,' the boy whispered, and the bird watched as the wind picked up his words and flew them into the sky.

The boy turned his face to the sun, as if he too could see his words catching on the wind, and his gaze fell upon the faded moon, still visible in the blue sky. He whistled for a while, then began to sing, 'Please let the moon that shines on me, shine on the ones I love.'

The pigeon cooed his happiness to the boy, and felt his feathers fluff around him as a woman walked her way towards the boy. She wore an old blue jacket, rough and worn, and she walked as though she beared a great pain on her shoulders, a great weariness. The woman had the same hair and eyes as the boy, and in her bag she carried an old wooden pigeon-racing clock. There was fear in the woman's eyes, but there was strength there too. The woman put her arm around the boy's shoulders. The boy did not smile, but he leaned his body just a bit closer towards the woman. She took the wooden box from her bag and they held it together, their fingertips touching, and they waited together.

The soft tint of peace fills the air around the pigeon, and he listens to the call of his flock rippling on the wind. He coos once, softly, the very beginning of a tune sung to him by a boy lost and alone, then the pigeon raises his wings into the sky, and lets the wind carry him home.

We are the ones that disappeared,
That ran, that got lost, that chose to go.
We are the ones tricked or chosen, sold or taken by
larger hands than ours.
We are the eyes that turned from the fist,
We are the feet that ran from the fear,
from the anger, from the pain, from the empty promise
of love and care.
We are the voices that whispered No.
We are the hands that could paint no more,
We are the minds that would not bend,
We are the bodies, trapped in fear, frozen and
limp,
We are the ones that smiled with our faces, but
cried rivers of blood from the dark of our souls.
We are the fingers that asked for a coin,
that pulled at a coat, that begged to be heard.
To be seen.
To exist.
So. So. So think on me when you sit to a meal,
When you point to a colour or smile at the
taste of a sweet picked in blood.
Talk to me when you turn from my voice,
Remember me when you say we all have
choices.
For I am the eyes that see into your soul
And I can never be silenced.

Esra Merkes, age 11

Author's Note

There are more people enslaved now than at any other time in human history. It is estimated that there are over 30 million people currently enslaved, and that more than a quarter of those people are children. That means there are more children enslaved right now than the entire child populations of Australia, New Zealand, Scotland and Wales put together. If every one of these children stood in a line holding hands, that line would stretch around the circumference of the earth *twice*, and then some.

These are not the children who are working for their families to help earn money in far off countries. This is not child labour. These are children who are exploited in a multitude of ways, forced to work inhumane hours in horrific conditions. These are children whose freedom has been taken from them. And this is happening in every single country in the world.

These are children who are forced to work in our restaurants and homes and markets and on our streets.

They are forced to work in brothels and marijuana factories, massage parlours and nail bars, garment factories and farms. They are forced into criminality and made to pay off absurd amounts of money, that many of them cannot hope to earn – ever. Some become victims of organ harvesting. These are children who are enslaved physically, financially, mentally and emotionally. And often, when they are found by police, these children are prosecuted, charged and imprisoned for taking part in illegal activities.

Children and adults being trafficked into slavery is not a new issue. Slavery is the fastest growing criminal industry in the world, generating over $150 billion every year. A recent EU report shows that children between the ages of six months and ten years old are usually sold for between €4000 and €8000. And yet, slavery is an issue that most of us are unaware of, and it is increasing at an alarming rate. Recent estimates suggest that more than 100 children are trafficked into the UK every week.

Children trafficked into slavery come from a variety of circumstances. Some are children who have left their homes of their own accord, some are children who have survived natural disasters and are left without adults to care for them. Some are from families in developing nations who are promised an education or an opportunity to help their families out of debt if they leave. Others are simply taken. With the ongoing refugee crisis, many unaccompanied refugee minors are now also being targeted by criminal gangs and trafficked into slavery. Tens of thousands of minors have gone missing from refugee camps, detention centres, shelters, foster homes and care homes. We have no idea where these children are. We have no idea what is happening to them. They are the ones that disappeared.

But the world doesn't have to be this way. On a recent trip to London, I stumbled upon a café that had an exhibition of photos of children living in refugee camps. There was a photo of an eleven-year-old girl with an accompanying quotation from her.

'You world, in spite of your vastness, and my littleness, I want to talk and raise my voice high.'

I hope one day we can live in a world in which all of us, whoever we are, no matter how small, can talk and raise our voices high. I hope one day we live in a world where we can all find the strength and courage to stand by our beliefs, and where every one of us, especially those most vulnerable, will be heard, and listened to.

I hope.

Acknowledgements

Thank you to all those people who found the courage and strength to tell their stories. Without you, this book would not be possible. And thank you to all the people who have made it possible for such stories to be told.

Thanks also to everyone at RCW literary agency, and an especially huge thank you to the wonderful Claire Wilson, who was, as always, invaluable in every way, despite being on leave. Thank you for all your support, encouragement and expert guidance. Thanks also to Rosie Price, who stepped in so effortlessly and took over Claire's role brilliantly.

Of course, this book would be nothing without the expertise of both Helen Thomas and Suzanne O'Sullivan, whose comments, advice, thoughts and reflections have made this book what it is today. I cannot express how much I delight in collaborating with you both.

Thanks also to everyone at Hachette and especially the teams at Orion Children's Books and Lothian. Thank you for all the support you have given me. I am honoured to be listed as one of your authors.

Thanks also to all my friends and family who have assisted and supported me along the way, and to my mother who enthusiastically reads each draft I send her way, and always helps me keep my perspective.

The biggest thanks of all goes to my amazing family, Mischa, Luca, Mani and Jugs. Without your help this book would never have made it. Thank you for solving each and every plot problem, for helping me discover my characters, for the endless jokes, and for assuring me that I always hate my books at some point in the drafting process. You are everything to me.

About the Author

Zana Fraillon is the author of several other books for young people including *The Bone Sparrow*, which was shortlisted for the *Guardian* Children's Fiction Prize 2016, the CILIP Carnegie Medal 2017 and won Book of the Year for Older Children at the Australia Book Industry Awards 2017. She lives in Victoria, Australia with her husband and three sons.

Zana was once told to 'shine a light in all the dark places'. Through her writing, she hopes to give voice to those who have been silenced, and enable us to see those who are hidden, balancing the realities of their situation with the power of hope and the strength of the human spirit.

You can follow her on Twitter @ZanaFraillon and visit her website at www.zanafraillon.com